Dealing with Mapinguari and Dogged Engineers

THE SORCERER'S GRIMOIRE
BOOK TWO

Tennis 2024!

AJ SHERWOOD

screenshot

This book is a work of fiction, so please treat it like a work of fiction. Seriously. References to real people, dead people, good guys, bad guys, stupid politicians, companies, restaurants, events, products, locations, pop culture references, or wacky historical events are intended to provide a sense of authenticity and are used fictitiously. Or because I wanted it in the story. Characters, names, story, location, dialogue, weird humor, and strange incidents all come from the author's very fertile imagination and are not to be construed as real. No, I don't believe in killing off main characters. Villains are a totally different story.

DEALING WITH MAPINGUARI AND DOGGED ENGINEERS

The Sorcerer's Grimoire Book 2

Copyright © 2024 by AJ Sherwood

Cover by Natasha Snow

vintage ornaments frame swirls and scrolls by Nimaxs/Shutterstock

All rights reserved.

No part of this book may be reproduced, scanned, or distributed in any printed or electronic form without permission. Please do not participate in or encourage electronic piracy of copyrighted materials in violation of the author's rights. NO AI/NO BOT. We do not consent to any Artificial Intelligence (AI), generative AI, large language model, machine learning, chatbot, or other automated analysis, generative process, or replication program to reproduce, mimic, remix, summarize, or otherwise replicate any part of this creative work, via any means: print, graphic, sculpture, multimedia, audio, or other medium. We support the right of humans to control their artistic works. (All typos are left on purpose to prove it's not AI written.)

Purchase only authorized editions.

www.ajsherwood.com

ONE

Adrien sat at his desk, ostensibly to pay bills, but really, he debated on whether or not to change into a different suit. Never mind that he'd changed three times already before even leaving his bedroom. Was the black suit too somber? With his black hair and pale skin, he sometimes worried that such a choice made him look like a ghoul. He didn't want to give the wrong impression to George and spoil everything.

No. Stop it. His choice of suit didn't matter one whit. He didn't know why he was so nervous about George calling on him this morning. Well, that was a lie, he did know. Of course he was nervous about trying to reconnect with someone who had unintentionally hurt him deeply. Relaxing his guard enough to trust George again would be quite the exercise.

The wound left behind by that night seven years ago still smarted, but Adrien wouldn't let pain make decisions for him. George had done everything he could to reach out, and Adrien wanted to believe in that sincerity.

He also very much wanted a proper family name for his boys' sake. The Danvers name carried great weight in the business world, and simply having it would open doors for them that might otherwise stay closed. Those kinds of connections would be vital in helping Julian and MacMallin in their careers and lives.

So despite Adrien's attack of nerves, he'd bought some small cakes from the bakery across the street, had MacMallin brew up some tea, and tried to mentally prepare himself for George's arrival.

Perhaps Julian and MacMallin had sensed his nerves, or shared them, as they'd taken special care in how they'd dressed. If looking their best allayed their fears, he wasn't about to tease the boys for it.

Despite anticipating George's arrival, Adrien's heart still leapt into his throat at the chime of the doorbell. He blew out a breath, thumped a palm over his heart to settle it back into its cavity, and went for the door.

MacMallin beat him there, opening it to reveal George Danvers. Adrien's cousin was dressed in a day suit of navy blue, which complemented his ginger hair nicely. The suit was obviously tailored to him, as it fit like a glove. Despite being thirty-two and a father of two, he looked younger today for some reason—more like a man in his early twenties. It could be the joy emanating from him that gave such an impression. Adrien, for his part, was relieved to see that joy. It soothed his nerves like a balm. George had a briefcase in hand, and he seemed quite as taken with MacMallin as the boy was with him. He stepped into the foyer, eyes solely on MacMallin as the door shut behind him. Darby circled around their feet, sniffing, tail wagging at this new person who had come to pet her.

George knew MacMallin's and Julian's history, thanks to his inquiries. Knew what they had been, what they'd been forced to do to survive, and Adrien found himself holding his breath and hoping George would not judge them for their past. One snide remark would end this relationship completely. Adrien would not tolerate anything short of love and acceptance for his boys.

George extended a hand. "Hello. I'm George, your new cousin. If I'm not wrong, you're MacMallin?"

Oh, thank god. Look at George's sincere smile, the relaxed body language. He meant every word.

MacMallin was good at reading people, and he took George's hand with a hesitant smile of his own. "Correct. It's very good to meet you, Cousin George."

"Likewise, likewise."

George turned, zeroed in on Adrien, and immediately wrapped him up in a fierce hug. It was unusual, to say the least; Adrien didn't remember George being this physically affectionate. But in that embrace, he could feel George's longing, the strong desire to have cherished family nearby, and he could only respond with the same fervor. He hugged his cousin, arms tight around his back, and soaked in the moment. Too long, he'd thought he'd lost this connection. Too long, he'd feared he'd never have his friend and cousin back.

"No more disappearing on me," George murmured against

his temple. "You hear?"

Adrien grinned against his shoulder. "I promise."

"Good." Only then did George release him and stand back.

Adrien straightened and gestured him in. "Don't stand there in the foyer, George. Come in, come in. We've tea set out at the table."

"Splendid." George came through, handing his hat over to MacMallin to hang up. "Could use a spot of tea. It's a rainy, chilly day outside."

Hearing the soft patter of Julian's footsteps, Adrien half turned toward the boy. "Proper introductions this time. This is Julian. Julian, George."

George once again extended a hand, and Julian took it, with a smile that looked strangely shy.

"Good to see you again, Julian. This time, as your new cousin. I must say, we're quite excited in the family to gain two such talented young men all at once." George leaned in a little, eyes bouncing between the boys, a smirk playing around his mouth. "According to another of our cousins, my uncle learned of you this past week and had an explosive temper tantrum because I'd adopted you both into my branch of the family. Which, truly, makes my year. He's a horrid sort of man."

For that matter, the news created petty joy in Adrien's heart. Anything that made his father upset brought some pep to his step.

Julian seemed unconcerned about a man he'd likely never meet. Instead, his expression was one of thinly veiled hope. "Are we...officially Danverses, then?"

"You are." George lifted the briefcase in illustration. "Just some loose ends to tidy up so we can get your passports."

Both boys looked fit to burst with happiness, and Adrien could not blame them. He felt the urge to hug them, almost checked the impulse with the current audience, then deliberately made the choice to follow through. His father had never shown him an ounce of physical affection, and he was determined to do the opposite of how he'd been raised. Hugs were part of that, awkward as it might feel at moments.

He reached out, drawing the boys in and hugging them about their waists. Their arms were tight around his waist and shoulders, and he sensed tears might be lurking—ones of pure joy. Perhaps some relief as well.

George surprised him by setting the briefcase down and putting a hand on both boys' shoulders, joining in on the embrace. It surprised the boys too, bringing their heads up and to the side, but honestly, it overjoyed Adrien that George would be so affectionate.

"You're proper Danverses now," George reiterated. "Which means holidays, family dinners, and once you're both old enough, a proper debut in society. My wife, Emily, is beside herself wanting to meet you. If it weren't for Sebastian's dental appointment, she'd have come with me today. We're not family in name only, keep that in mind. We want to get to know you. You're truly welcome anytime you wish to visit."

A feather could have knocked Adrien off his feet. He'd truly expected the adoption to be one in name only. An olive branch, if you would, to mend a broken relationship. He'd never once considered George had *actually meant it*.

"But..." Julian faltered, shooting Adrien a panicked glance. "But sir, we were—"

"You are children," George said, voice firm, a hardness entering his eyes. "Children adults utterly failed to provide for or protect. Make no mistake about it, I do not have any intention of holding your past against you, as it wasn't your choice in the first place. What I see before me are two bright young men who have all the potential in the world, ones I'm quite proud to call family. And if anyone ever says different, I want their name and direction, and I'll have very sharp words for them."

Well. When George did something, he certainly didn't do it by half measures. Adrien was thrilled at this. If George stuck to his guns, then Adrien would have no qualms about leaving the boys with him if necessity struck.

MacMallin looked George dead in the eye for a long moment, as if ascertaining his sincerity, then the tension in his shoulders bled out. "I'll hold you to that, Cousin."

"Do. Now, let's go sit. I'm sure the tea will get cold at this rate."

Adrien was happy to move the location to the kitchen even if George was wrong. He had spells on his kettles. Tea didn't dare grow cold in his flat. He shooed the boys on ahead of him, following their lead into the kitchen.

They all took a moment to settle, pouring tea and doctoring

it to their preferences, passing around the small petit fours, and so on. To Adrien's great amusement, Darby chose to lie on top of George's feet. She apparently liked him. George, on his part, shared the amusement and did nothing to disturb the pup.

"However did you acquire your dog?" George regarded the tricolor collie with interest. "We've been talking about getting the children a dog. This one seems quite a good-tempered one."

George had hit upon the favorite topic of both boys, and MacMallin was quick to fill him in. "She's amazing. Very sweet and smart. Jules got her as a reward for a job."

Not expecting this, George blinked at him. "A reward? Julian, are you taking on separate jobs already?"

Holding up both hands to stave off such a thought, Julian shook his head. "No such thing. I was assisting Master. You know the disaster that hit Portsmouth? When the kraken attacked earlier this year?"

"Ah, yes, I'd read of it in the paper. You were part of the cleanup, then?"

"We were, yes. There's a woman who breeds collies, and she asked for our help. Her dog had given birth but was trapped in the garden behind a fallen mast. Master and I got all the dogs safely out and repaired her house, and she gave me a puppy in thanks."

Knowing George would be amused by this, Adrien threw in, "Cynric got one too."

"Ha! Of course he did." George chuckled before selecting another small cake. "You two don't know this, but I know your master's friends quite well. They used to holiday with us every year, for at least one of the major holidays. I'm not surprised in the slightest that Cynric got jealous and wanted a puppy too. Huge animal lover, that one. As bad as you, Adrien."

Adrien shrugged in agreement, as truly that was the case. He'd not had a pet before this simply because he was forever hopping about the globe.

Julian asked hesitantly, "How is Sebastian? No ill effects from that curse, I hope?"

George seemed pleased with the question, his smile growing. "Nothing of the sort, thanks to you and Adrien. He recovered quickly after you treated him. No, his appointment today was a problem of another sort. A tooth not growing in properly. A little dental work, a potion, and he'll be fine. Poor tyke was in some pain from it, hence why Emily rushed him in."

"Good." Julian relaxed back into his chair. "It was my first case dealing with a person's health."

"Was it? Well, you did fine. For that matter, you've not been apprenticed long with Adrien and only recently debuted. How goes your studies?"

Adrien watched as George spoke with both boys, getting to know them better, and felt like his heart grew three sizes too large for his chest. He never thought he'd see the likes of this. He'd gained his family back, even if only in part, and it was a joyous thing indeed.

"Well, I must say, you're both learning quickly." George gave a pleased nod. "Adrien said you were brilliant, and I do see now what he meant by that. I'd had half a mind to talk you out of taking them to Brazil, Adrien, as it seemed a bit too soon for them to leave the country for a case. But I won't now. I think traveling the world will do them good."

"Glad you agree with me," Adrien drawled.

"Don't take that tone with me, you rascal. In any case, I won't ask you to repeat the details, as Emily will ask you all the same questions, but do give me the basics for your trip."

"Will I meet Emily soon, then?"

"I'd hoped you'd have dinner with us next week. She's dying to meet you all."

Adrien didn't even need to think twice on this offer. "Tell me the day and time and we'll be there."

"Splendid! Now, back to the trip. I'll need some information for the passports. You'll leave when?"

"Two weeks from now. Or so I hope. Hugh's been neck-deep in a project, and he says he must finish that before we sail."

George drew paperwork out of his briefcase but paused after placing the papers on the table, giving Adrien an arch look.

He couldn't fathom why that expression graced his cousin's face. "What?"

"Hugh, is it?"

Oh, hell. Look at George leaping to all the wrong conclusions. "We're friends, George. Friends can be on a first-name basis."

George didn't buy that. He looked to the boys. "I want a second opinion. Is this man handsome?"

"Very much so," Julian confirmed with a teasing grin at

Adrien. "And I think he's very interested in Master."

Oh, for fuck's sake, not them too. "Do cease and desist. We're talking of passports and travel."

"If you say so." George smirked at the boys, as if to say *We'll discuss this more later*.

Which was precisely what Adrien feared. MacMallin and Julian kept urging him to open up to Hugh, but he just couldn't bear to do so. Hugh was such an amazing man and friend, and Adrien didn't want to jeopardize that. Utterly refused to do so, in fact.

He firmly nipped this teasing in the bud. "Now, along with the dates of departure and possible return, what else do you need?"

Two

For the next week, Adrien went about the logistics of getting ready for departure. Since he would be gone for possibly several months, he paid all the bills in advance, with authorization to pull from his account if necessary. Then he bought new luggage for the boys, did the paperwork with George for IDs and passports, et cetera, et cetera. In between all of that, he juggled magic and school lessons. Adrien wondered how parents around the world managed to do all of this and actually sleep.

It was honestly a delight to go to George's for dinner that evening because at least he didn't need to think about yet another meal. It wasn't until they arrived at the residence that Adrien's nerves set in. The boys were visibly nervous—though for a different reason—now that they'd arrived in the most respectable section of London at an earl's townhouse. It might not have fully sunk in until this moment, what it meant to be a Danvers.

Well, not that Adrien could blame either boy for their reaction. Only one week had passed since being adopted; that was hardly enough time to settle into their new identities. It felt like Julian and MacMallin had held their breath until Adrien had signed the documents, finalizing everything. Even Adrien had moments of feeling like it all might have been a dream. He could only imagine how his boys felt, gaining a proper family of their own.

Adrien did know them to be thrilled, however, if the numerous questions he'd been peppered with were any indication. He'd also found multiple sheets with them practicing their new signatures, some of them with hearts dancing around the Danvers name. With all the repetition, their names now looked more like signatures and less like chicken scratch.

Both boys were very carefully dressed in their best for tonight's dinner. Julian looked quite sharp in a pale grey suit, his blond hair in a gentle wave about his face that Adrien knew for a fact took three hair products to manage. MacMallin wore a dark green suit, white shirt starched within an inch of its life, his newly cut dark hair lying in loose curls. They looked every inch the respectable Danvers children that they now were.

Exiting the carriage, Adrien straightened his jacket and took a deep breath before heading up the front steps. He didn't even get to knock on the door before it abruptly opened. Taft stood there, silver hair gleaming in the entryway's light, smartly turned out as usual, narrow face alight with joy. "Master Adrien."

"Taft, you old devil, it's a delight to see you." Adrien clasped the man's hand in a strong grip, grinning up at him. He'd truly missed the man and felt some of his nerves melt away. "You're well? How's Sara?"

"We're both in the pink of health," Taft assured him. "You're under orders to see Sara tonight before you leave. I am given to understand heads will roll otherwise. But who's with you? Our new charges?"

"Indeed. Julian, MacMallin, this is Benedict Taft. He's been with the Danvers family since before...well, any of us younger generation were born, certainly. He's more an honorary uncle to me than the family butler. Taft, my apprentices and newly minted cousins."

Taft held out a hand to Julian first, his smile kind. "A pleasure to finally meet you, Master Julian."

Apparently overwhelmed, Julian managed to accept the handshake and stutter back, "Ah, a pleasure, sir."

"Master MacMallin."

"Mac, please," MacMallin said, trying to be suave but also looking somewhat shell-shocked.

"Come in, sirs," Taft said, taking their coats. "Dinner will be another fifteen minutes."

"Taft, are they here?" a woman's voice called out from the drawing room.

"Indeed, my lady," Taft called back.

A swish of skirts heralded the entrance of the woman who had to be George's wife, Emily. She was not the stunning beauty Adrien had expected. Instead, she had rambunctiously curled blonde hair, an upturned nose, and a heart-shaped face that made her "cute" rather than pretty. Then her face lit up in a smile and Adrien trashed his appraisal of her completely, as that expression made her instantly captivating. "Excellent. George!"

"Coming, dearest!" George said with some exasperation from somewhere upstairs. He came down the elegantly curved staircase and into the tiled foyer, already dressed for dinner in a neat black suit.

Emily, too impatient to wait for her husband, stepped forward with hands outstretched. "I'm Emily Danvers. Welcome, truly. Not just to dinner, but to the family."

"Thank you," Adrien said.

Finally arriving on scene, George took up the introductions. "Emily, this is Adrien."

"Lovely to meet you." Emily greeted him with a very curious once-over.

Adrien always got that expression upon first introductions, mostly because he didn't resemble George in the slightest. His Thai mother had much to do with that, as he pulled strongly from her genetics. "Enchanted, Cousin. This is Julian and MacMallin."

Grasping their hands in each of hers, Emily beamed at the boys. "Welcome. Oh, you're handsome, both of you. George, for shame, you could have mentioned that."

George rolled his eyes while smiling at his wife. "Yes, dearest. Let's not leave them standing in the foyer."

Emily pulled one of each of the boys' arms through the crooks of her own, escorting them. They were definitely startled but didn't fight her, following along. "You come with me to the drawing room, I have a million questions to ask both of you. I understand you're catching up on your studies, yes? Who's tutoring you?"

As they went off, the boys answering, George caught Adrien's shoulder and stalled him. With a weather eye on his wife's retreating back, he lowered his voice and said, "She's intensely excited to have them in the family."

"I can tell." Her enthusiasm had already bowled his apprentices over, but the experience would be good for them. They needed a maternal figure in their lives. Anastasia inhabited more of a big sister role for them, and Adrien wasn't at all interested in interfering. Emily, he had the feeling, would fill the motherly role nicely.

"I did receive a letter from your father this morning," George said in the same low voice. His face screwed up in a distasteful frown. "Just as I'd heard, he's quite irate at the whole thing. I sent a letter back telling him where he could put his asinine opinions. But still, I expect he won't let it rest there and will come at you eventually."

"I'll be gone to Brazil in eight days and will probably be down there for three months. He'll have turned his attention to something else by the time we return."

"Hopefully so. Still, I thought I should warn you."

"I do appreciate it." Sensing he shouldn't leave the other three alone much longer, Adrien made his way into a very well-appointed drawing room. It had clearly been remodeled recently. Everything was done in a modern style, with graphic symmetry, repeated patterns on the upholstery, and an abstract oil painting hanging above the fireplace. It was somewhat at odds with the traditional look of the townhouse's architecture. It had been done in the Roman style, but that was hardly for Adrien to comment on, so he bit his tongue.

"Where are the children?" Adrien had fully expected them to be here since it was a family dinner.

"Both down with colds," George said with a sigh. "Poor tykes. They can't seem to get a respite from illnesses this year. We put them to bed early. Unfortunate timing, as they were so looking forward to meeting their new cousins."

"Ah. Well, I hope they recover quickly."

"So do we. They are not the best at staying still."

Emily had Julian and MacMallin on the couch with her, one boy to either side. They looked overwhelmed by all her questions, but they were smiling genuinely at her. Adrien observed for a moment, slow to find his own seat. She was sincerely interested in what they were saying; it showed in her every gesture and expression, and his apprentices genuinely responded to that. They were much more at ease than Adrien had expected them to be five minutes into this dinner party.

When he took a chair across from them, Emily looked up at him and demanded, "Are you truly trying to teach them instead of sending them to school? As well as train Julian in magic?"

She sounded so miffed on their behalf that Adrien took no umbrage at the accusation. "My dear cousin, what do you suggest I do? Putting them into a school will do them no good at this point. Their peers have years of education already. They'd be quite quickly lost."

"I expect you to use good common sense and hire a tutor," she said in exasperation. "If you don't know of one, I can recommend several."

When he'd first acquired the boys, he'd put off doing so because he'd feared a tutor judging them for their street manners, or worse, learning of their pasts. They'd learned enough at this point to avoid such scrutinization. "I'd be very interested in their contact information," Adrien said. "In truth, I think a tutor will do a better job, as the boys would have dedicated times to study without me ducking out every five minutes to attend to business." He'd just have to be very, very careful in the interviews.

"That's settled, then, I'll fetch their information for you before you leave tonight. And when are you buying MacMallin new clothes? Look at his sleeves, they're an inch too short on him. Never mind, I'll take them shopping myself tomorrow. They can't go to Brazil with you without properly fitting clothes, it simply won't do."

George gave him an I-told-you-so look Adrien pretended not to see. "I'd be very grateful if you did. There's quite a few arrangements I still must see to before we depart."

"Good, then it's settled."

Taft stood in the doorway and informed them, "Dinner is served."

They retreated from the drawing room and went across to the dining room, taking seats as their hostess directed. Adrien ended up with Emily to his right, the boys across from them, and George at the head of the table. They were served a very excellent tomato soup to start them off. Adrien was of the opinion that anything he didn't have to cook improved in taste by at least fifty percent.

"Adrien," Emily said, her spoon hovering in the white china bowl, "you mentioned your client for the Brazil trip is once again Sir Hugh Quartermain?"

"Indeed he is." Adrien paused in eating to answer more fully. "In fact, he inquired if I could help him just as we finished that fiasco at the Isle of Man. It sounds quite an interesting problem, and he's become rather a friend, so I took it on."

"What is the problem, exactly?" Emily asked.

"I've yet to get all the specifics, but as he explained things to me, there's a resource he wants in Brazil. He's tried sending in work crews to mine it out, but he's hit a roadblock of sorts.

Something nearby keeps killing the workers. He's not sure if it's the work of some creature—Brazil is chock-full of dangerous sorts—a curse, or if it's a rival posing as a native monster. Either way, he can't convince anyone else to go in there. He's tried hiring local sorcerers, but to no good effect. He said no one worth their salt would take on the job."

"Hence you." George patted his lips with a napkin and nodded for the soup's removal to a servant hovering nearby. "I'm surprised you don't have all the particulars when you're so close to leaving."

"We fully intended to meet before now and exchange information," Adrien admitted sourly, "but he's had some trouble making time. There's quite a bit he has to sign off on, apparently, to free up the time necessary to take us down there. But we've an appointment for lunch tomorrow. I hope to have all the details then."

"You'll have to tell us the tale when you return from overseas," George encouraged. He turned to MacMallin and added, "I understand you toured a new factory Sir Hugh built?"

"Yes, sir," MacMallin said, already warming to his subject. "Amazing, that was. He explained the process, generally, and even showed me one of the machine's inner workings, as they were having issues with it."

"Are all his factories dedicated to producing Remedium 11?" Emily asked curiously, shoving her soup bowl aside. Clearly she had more interest in conversing than eating. "I understand that's Sir Hugh's main enterprise."

"The first factory I toured with him produced it, but not all of them," MacMallin said. "He told me that he's most famous for his Remedium 11 production, but that's not the only thing he produces. His factory in Exeter has a line for electric blankets."

George blinked. "Heavens, I've heard of those. Dangerous, aren't they?"

"Only if left on for more than four hours, or so he tells me," MacMallin explained earnestly. "He said they've got some fail-safes built in now so they don't run as dangerously hot. But they're perfect to use for people who have poor circulation in their legs. Those who are confined to wheelchairs or have had strokes, that sort of thing. He said, too, that they can be used by people in very cold climates, like Russia, where there's not enough heat."

"Well. That is very clever."

"He said the first one was invented by a gentleman in America. Sir Hugh bought the rights to produce it over here. He said even with paying the patent fees, he'll make a mint."

Of that, Adrien had no doubt. Hugh had the unique talent of turning lead into gold.

Emily smiled at MacMallin. "He sounds like a wonderful gentleman, and I hope to meet him. I've only heard lovely things about him."

"He's very kind," Julian chipped in. "He looked out for us during the last case, even helped us when Master was injured."

George snapped about to look at Adrien with concern. "You were injured?"

Growling at his unapologetic apprentice, Adrien answered in resignation. "I'm fine. Another colleague was on hand to heal me. Really, Julian, that wasn't necessary to add to the conversation."

With a shrug, Julian applied himself to the delicate fish that was placed in front of him.

In an attempt to turn the tide of the conversation, Adrien asked, "George, is it still the plan for us to come spend part of August at your country estate? For the Summer Bank Holiday?"

"Yes, of course," George said, although the dark look he aimed at Adrien promised they were not finished with that conversation. "You, my new cousins, and hopefully your new lover."

Adrien nearly choked on his fish. "What lover?!"

"Oh, you don't have one? I could have sworn George mentioned someone..." Emily sounded strangely disappointed. She patted Adrien's arm consolingly. "It's fine, you're a handsome man. I've no doubt you'll meet someone soon."

He regarded her with the strangest look, quite certain she'd taken leave of her senses. Since when was his love life of any interest to Emily? "You've more faith in that than I do, apparently."

"Come now, Adrien," Emily chided warmly. "You're barely twenty-five, you can't throw in the towel for romance already. You're a famous man. Surely other men take notice of you."

"Congratulations," he said. His skin was tight with either embarrassment or tension, he couldn't discern which. "This is by far the most bizarre dinner conversation I've ever been privy to."

Giggling, Emily went back to eating her fish. "I'll spare you anything further tonight. But do understand that we want you to be comfortable with us in that aspect of your life."

"Us too?" MacMallin blurted out, eyes going wide at his slip.

Emily blinked at him. "Yes, of course. Oh, is your nature like Adrien's?"

MacMallin cast a quick glance at Adrien, questioning, to which Adrien gave a shrug. Apparently it really was safe to talk about such matters here. Squarely, MacMallin faced her and said, "I actually prefer both boys and girls."

"Oh." Nonplussed, Emily took a second to process his words. "How interesting. I've never met someone with that inclination before. You will have to tell me what attracts you to both. You too, Julian. I'm quite interested but rather naïve about the whole matter. No one really talks about such things, unfortunately. It leaves me with more questions than answers. Perhaps tomorrow, during our outing, we can find a moment to talk about it properly."

Adrien considered the possible conversation tomorrow between a duke's illegitimate daughter and two former prostitutes. Hopefully Emily wasn't very shockable. The boys really didn't know how to phrase things delicately sometimes.

They might not have understood her open curiosity, but certainly they liked that she wanted to know more. Julian beamed a smile at her that was likely to turn even a monk's head. "I'd love to. There's so many preconceptions and rumors, and half of it is bunk."

"Isn't that always the way of it?" Emily bemoaned to him, sympathetic. "Then do tell me everything tomorrow. George's ears burn when I get too frank with him sometimes."

George gave a long-suffering sigh and focused on his fish.

On the other hand, maybe it was George who Adrien should worry for.

Having pity, Emily changed the subject. "Let's talk about holiday plans. Boys, have you ever gone fishing? No? George adores doing it, as does Sebastian. You should try it at least once. There's a pond at the back of George's estate—"

Adrien let the conversation roll on for a moment, drinking a healthy gulp of red wine to help steady his nerves. He simply was not accustomed to his family—especially a family member he'd just met—so casually asking about his love life. It was heartening, in a sense, that she would be so open about discussing it. And it lent credence to George's invitation, that Adrien was welcome to bring a lover with him for the holiday season, but…it still felt remarkably strange.

The best sort of strange. A smile quirking his lips, he forced himself to relax and enjoy a rare family dinner.

Three

Hugh sat at his desk doing paperwork.

It was the one aspect of his career he disliked because most of it was very dull and routine in the worst of ways. But tonight it especially grated on him, and he wasn't quite sure why.

Well, now, that was the falsehood of the ages. He knew precisely why.

It had been two weeks since he'd seen Adrien, Julian, MacMallin, and Darby. Two very long weeks. Staying busy with his various businesses kept his mind off them for a time, but it didn't help when he came home to a quiet, dark home every evening. The time had seemed to drag, each day only emphasizing what he didn't have. He'd see them tomorrow, and that idea filled him with excitement, but it would also be a fleeting reunion. Only lunch together before separating once again. Part of his heart soared with the idea of at least seeing them briefly. The other part longed for more.

His pen stopped on the paper. He lifted it before it could leave a stain, then sighed heavily.

How could he possibly focus on work when all he wanted was a chance? A chance to win the love of that beautiful, intelligent, captivating man. Adrien was the epitome of a dream, who every person aspired to have as a partner. Hugh freely admitted he'd been attracted from the first moment. Spending time with Adrien had only cemented the interest.

Add in two teenagers and an adorable puppy and Hugh had been head over heels before he could even think to guard his heart.

His London flat felt so empty without them, which was nonsensical because they'd never been in this flat to begin with. Still, he yearned to have them here. The flat wasn't large by any means, but it felt cavernous tonight and as still as the grave.

A key turning in the lock was a welcome sound, and Hugh

hastily got up from the desk, coming around it to see who entered through the front door. It could only be one of two people: his mother or his master. Both were always welcome, but tonight especially he could use the company.

It was his mother, Magda, a basket in her hands, her hair a darker red than when he'd last seen her. Hugh had come by his copper hair honestly. His mother's turned white with each passing season, but she combated this with hair dye, refusing to let the white strands win.

She also had her nails done, makeup on, and was in a very smart maroon dress he'd never seen before. It always did his heart good to see her dressed up like this. She'd worked so hard to support them when he was a child, and her now living a life of luxury felt like the best gift he could ever give her.

"You look stunning, Mother," Hugh said, coming to take the basket from her and giving her a kiss on either cheek. "Were you out on a special occasion?"

"I thank ye for the compliment, it be rare at me age. As for the occasion, Lily's baby shower was today," she reminded him.

The neighbors he'd grown up with were practically family, Lily being the oldest daughter. They'd banded together while living in London's slums, and it was a bond not forgotten, even now when the Quartermains were much better off financially. "Was it? You gave her a present in my name, I hope."

"I did. A cradle with that self-rocking machine ye created. She be thrilled. Sent me home with cakes and such for ye."

"Oh, is that what's in the basket?" The smells wafting out were rather enticing.

"Come, let's sit, have tea, and chat. I havenae seen ye in weeks."

"Yes, well, I've been rather busy." He escorted her into the kitchen, setting the basket on the table before filling the kettle.

His kitchen was a very lonely space, with nothing more than the bare essentials in it. It also needed a good coat of paint on the cabinets, but he wasn't worried about it. The flat was a space he came to when he needed to sleep, that was all.

His mother doffed her coat and hat, then sat at the table, looking him over with a keen eye. "Just as well I popped round. Ye seem to be in a sorry mood."

He joined her at the table, grimacing. "I can't disagree. Feeling sorry for myself, that's all it is. I'm not making the sort of headway I wish."

"Which project be this?"

His mother was always a good listening ear, and often he could tell her the problem and find the solution on his own. Just the act of slowing down, speaking it into the air, gave him the right perspective to figure it out.

That said… "It's, um, not a business project that has me stumped."

She lit up with an expression of pure glee. "Ye've found a man ye like."

"I have," he said, a little shy for some reason.

She slapped the table, hooting with laughter. "Finally! Right, so tell me everythin', leave no detail out. Be he handsome?"

"Handsome…isn't the right word. Stunningly beautiful is a better descriptor. He's half-Thai, half-English, born here in England but he lives in Thailand most of the time. From what I've gathered, he's multilingual, truly an incredibly brilliant man." Warming up to his topic, which granted didn't take much, his words picked up speed. "The sorcerer I hired to help me in Isle of Man, that's who I'm speaking of."

"Adrien Danvers." Her mouth formed a perfect "O" in understanding. "Ha! I teased he might be handsome, but here ye be, smitten already. Oh my. Son, ye really do have good taste. I heard all about how much he did at the isle. Our kin be singing his praises. Said it would have been a disaster if he hadnae be there."

"They're correct, it would have been. I admire his magical prowess, it's formidable in its own right, but I wish you could meet him. It's his heart that made me fall for him. He has the kindest, most giving heart. He took in two lads off the streets to train and raise. They're incredibly good boys, Mother. In fact, I'll take on one of them as my own apprentice."

She clapped her hands together, excitement almost sending her out of her chair. "What's his name? Ye think he's a good fit for the trade?"

"MacMallin, and yes, he's got the gift for engineering. It's like watching myself at a young age. He instinctively *kens*, you know?"

"Oh blessed be, I kept hoping ye'd find a good apprentice to pass yer hard work on to."

"I have as well. But I'd never have met him without Adrien.

For it was Adrien who rescued him first, gave him the education and chance to become anything he wanted." Knowing this would convince her as nothing else would, he added, "He got a collie for the boys, too. So they could have a dog."

"Sold!" Mother gave a firm nod. "Anyone who knows the value of a dog be good in me books. Be he interested in ye at all?"

"I don't know, and that's the rub." Hugh massaged his temples, feeling like a headache might be incoming.

The kettle went off with a shrill whistle. He almost got up to fetch it, but his mother waved him back down again, popping up and heading for the kettle.

"Is he not like ye, then? Doesnae like men?"

"No, I'm told he does. But I think he's been hurt before. He's incredibly guarded, defensive when there's no need to be. My dating history might be sparse, but I do believe his was horrid."

She brought the kettle and cups back to the table with her, a pinched frown stretching her lips thin. "I dinnae like the sound of that at all. He be a sweet man, from all descriptions, and yet other men used him ill? There be no fairness in this world."

"No, indeed there is not." In the interest of full disclosure, he said with a wince, "And his family disowned him for his inclinations."

Magda turned her head in slow, creaking degrees, jaw dropping. "WHAT?!"

Hugh was equally irate, so he could only grunt in sour agreement.

His mother let loose a string of curses most sailors would pause to admire. "No parent should shun a child over something like *that*. What be wrong with this world? And him such a good man, too."

Thanks to his mother, Hugh knew what true unconditional love was. Hugh was forever thankful for her. Otherwise, he'd not be the man he was today.

"I'm just as mad. I've tried reassuring him that I don't think differently of him because of his nature, and that went over rather well. He at least dropped his guard somewhat around me. But I can't seem to reach his heart fully."

"Could he be guarded and defensive because o' his boys?"

Now there was a good question. "Perhaps? He trusts me with them, though. Enough to let me have MacMallin as an apprentice."

"True." She poured tea into the cups, still frowning. "Son, I can speak from experience that dating while raising a child be a much more difficult thing. Ye dinnae want to give yer heart out readily because ye know the impact ye will have on yer child. It could well be his instincts are at war."

"How do I prove myself?"

"Time. Sincerity." She gave him a speaking look as she passed a cup over. "Sincerity wins hearts more than anything else. Ye dinnae need to do anythin' flashy, but steadily prove ye will always stand by him, and help with the boys when he needs it. Even when he doesnae need it. Ye be a handsome lad. I think once ye prove yer sincerity, ye'll be fine."

"You might be a bit biased," Hugh pointed out, even as he smiled at her.

"Of course I be, I be yer mother, but it be true nonetheless. When will ye start properly chasing the man?"

"Tomorrow." Hugh was sure on that part, at least. Even if it made him anxious. He so desperately wanted to get this right on the first try. "I'm to have lunch with him and the boys."

"Good. A good man like that, he willnae be single forever." She took a sip of tea and gave a satisfied sigh. "It be quite the pretty package ye've found yerself, with a good-hearted man, sweet children, and even a cute pupper thrown in. Dinnae let moss grow, but dinnae let haste and impatience ruin it for ye. There be no deadline here, *a chuilein*."

It was sound advice. Advice he'd needed to hear, as he had felt a touch impatient. "Thanks. I'll do my best."

"And the second ye feel it safe, I want ta meet them."

He gave her a speaking look in return. "You were saying about impatience…?"

"Do as I say, not as I do," she retorted primly. "Bring the pup too."

Now that, he should have expected.

FOUR

Adrien had set the lunch appointment at his favorite club, The Grimoire. It was known amongst the magical community for its discretion. Nearly as old as the city itself, it sat in the very heart of London, a four-story building that sprawled out over half of the block. Only two main doors faced the street, both of them for show, as they had more locking spells and wards on them than anyone could count at a glance. The side entrance, a discreet and simple door, was the way members chose to enter and leave. It looked unremarkable to the naked eye—a simple mahogany door with brass latches. However, it was in fact the most hideously complex magic Adrien had ever laid eyes on. It was warded and spelled so that only a member or their guest could pass the threshold. The doorman posted outside was an old war veteran, stocky and curt, missing half the fingers on his left hand due to some conflict in India. He was fundamentally incapable of smiling, although he softened a mite seeing the three of them approach. At least, he looked less inclined to beat them bloody. "Sorcerer Danvers."

"Sampson. How are you faring today?"

"Fine, thank you, sir." Sampson softened another touch before nodding to the boys. "Julian, MacMallin. Rare to see you here."

"We're preparing to go off to Brazil," Julian said, unable to tamp down on his excitement. "Master encouraged us to sit in on the meeting."

"I see. Brazil, is it?" Putting two and two together, Sampson asked brusquely, "You've a guest coming then, sir?"

"Sir Hugh Quartermain. And he's rarely late, so he'll likely be here directly."

"I'll escort him in, sir."

"I appreciate that, Sampson, thank you." Adrien slipped him a tip as Sampson opened the door for them.

When Adrien had first seen the inside of The Grimoire at age ten, he'd been so impressed by the foyer that he'd stood and stared at it for a good minute before his master caught his collar and dragged him along. The adult version of him had more control over himself, but it remained impressive. The club looked like a cathedral on the inside, complete with stained glass windows, arching balustrades, and suits of armor lining the tiled mosaic floor. It had a very medieval theme inside. It looked pretty enough, but Adrien knew that if some trouble went down, the suits of armor would become animated and attack, the glass windows would come down like a jail cell, and the spells along the floor would tamp down any sorcerer who attempted to use magic. It was eye-catching decor, no mistake, but deadly to the unwary or unwise.

They went up a flight of wide, creaking stairs to the second level, where the dining room was. Adrien chose a random table to sit at, waiting on Hugh. They'd barely settled before he arrived, striding through the doors confidently, his eyes immediately finding them.

Adrien had done his best to not think of Hugh for two solid weeks and had ultimately failed. Seeing him now, he was hit with a keen yearning, like a chasm in his chest aching to be filled. He'd missed the man, and there was no denying it. Adrien's eyes drank him in, unable to do otherwise. Hugh looked good, his tall and stocky frame in a rich green suit, flattering his short, burnished copper hair and tanned skin. He looked, quite frankly, good enough to eat, and Adrien had to quell several instincts and remind himself that they were strictly friends.

"Hello, Adrien, Julian, Mac. I say, first time I've been in the place, but it's damn impressive inside."

Julian, smiling, popped up to shake his hand. "Glad you could make it, sir."

"Me too, lad. It's been a right business convincing my employees to let go of me these days." Hugh shook all their hands, then looked about. "I'm half famished, actually. Where's a waiter?"

"There's a host there who we can order from, or you can choose anything from the buffet," Adrien said, pointing in the appropriate directions. "Either way, the food is excellent. It's why I recommended the place."

"Buffet," Hugh said decisively.

Having no objection to that, they all went and filled up their plates, the boys practically mounding theirs over. They discussed no business as they ate, and the boys went up for seconds before Hugh's hunger slackened enough that he sat back with a satisfied sigh. "That was excellent. Shame I can't be a member here."

"Anytime you wish to dine here, I'll take you." Adrien had almost thought better of it than to offer, but dammit all, they were friends. It wouldn't be strange to say this, surely? Not giving himself time to linger on the thought, he gestured to the table in general—not that it was a large group with two adults and two apprentices. "All right, Hugh. You've our undivided attention. What is in Brazil that you're so eager to get your hands on?"

"Manganese," Hugh said.

Adrien let out a soft "ah" of understanding.

MacMallin lifted a hand. "Not following, sir."

For his sake, Hugh explained patiently. "Manganese is a mineral found in several foods. Nuts, for instance. Teas, some whole grains, and several leafy green vegetables. It's an essential nutrient for the body and a vital ingredient for medicines. It's also very important in the manufacture of industrial metal alloys, particularly in steel. It's unfortunately not usually found as a free element in nature. In fact, we normally find it in combination with iron. And Brazil, specifically an area called Pará, has the largest deposit I've ever set eyes on."

Adrien hadn't known about the alloy. He'd assumed Hugh would need it for medicinal purposes, as that was the man's main stock-in-trade. "How far into the Amazon is this collection of manganese?"

"Roughly five hundred kilometers," Hugh said dryly. "Which is part of the problem, certainly. It's not too far off the beaten path from the main river that leads into the Amazon Rainforest, which is…problematic in a different sense if one isn't careful."

"I would think being next to a river would make things easier…" Julian trailed off, a light coming on. "Oh. Is there something in the river?"

"And out of the river," Hugh said, sounding resigned on several levels. "There are at least two creatures that cargo crews regularly encounter, and I don't even want to tell you of the other creatures I've heard about. Brazil seems as chock-full of mythical races as any European country. Worse, in some ways, as Brazil seems intent on importing more from the other cultures that live there."

Seeing that Hugh had lost the boys again, Adrien pitched in to explain. "Brazil was conquered and made a Portuguese colony for a long time until roughly a hundred years ago, when they declared their independence. Because of so much outside influence, you have the Voodoo beliefs from the Black slaves, the Catholic beliefs, the indigenous myths, the Asian myths, and I could continue on. The culture is very much a hodgepodge of mythologies, religions, and so forth. Not all creatures are locked into regions. Remember, some of them can function anywhere assuming they have enough people with a strong belief system in the area."

Julian and MacMallin shared a look. "I now understand the problem," MacMallin muttered to himself.

"Well, no, there's more," Hugh said, sipping his drink. "I wish it was that simple. The indigenous people are accustomed to working around all these native creatures. They know the right precautions to take. When I initially surveyed the area, my guides mentioned there were some things that were nuisances, but I wouldn't encounter any real danger if we took the right safety measures. After I left, that's when the trouble started. There is some sort of unknown creature—or creatures, the reports aren't clear—that has taken up residence near my worksite. Or what should be my worksite. It kills anything that comes near the area. I've sent telegraphs requesting a hunting party only to lose the entire party. I can't get a local sorcerer in there at all, despite my numerous requests. They refuse to go anywhere near the rainforest, say it's bad juju."

Adrien knew very well the breed of sorcerers in Brazil. They were equally divided between the highly competent and the charlatans, much like the sorcerers in England. Suspecting what had actually happened, he asked, "Tell me, Hugh, how good is your Portuguese?"

"I know enough to order food, buy things in the market, and insult someone's mother," he answered bluntly.

"So when you went looking for a local sorcerer to hire...?" Adrien said, his suggestive tone filling in the end of that sentence.

Hugh shrugged. "I likely didn't get anyone competent responding to me. Yes, I'm quite aware. The language barrier is part of the problem. But my business partner, Ribeiro, is a native and even he couldn't find a sorcerer willing to go in there. All of them were too superstitious to even entertain the thought. I can't spend months on end in the country helping sort through people until I find the right person for the job. It's much easier for me to take you to the problem."

Adrien couldn't fault the logic—Hugh was exactly right. "I've not had to travel by ship to the South American region before. The last time I went, we were portaled by my master, who'd had access to a permanent portal. Tell me, what will be our port and how long do you expect travel to take?"

"About twenty days, more or less." Hugh had a thoughtful expression. "And ships only go to port in Rio de Janeiro. I wish differently, as we're headed for Macapá, which will be the most direct passage for us to Pará by riverboat. So from Rio, we'll have to sail up to Macapá and then take the river in the rest of the way to the worksite, which is an abandoned village. So, about thirty days in total for travel, one way. Assuming the weather doesn't turn foul on us."

Adrien had not realized it took that long to reach their destination; he'd expected it to be a little shorter than that. "Hugh, I'm not at all inclined to portal the four of us from London to Pará. Even with mithril to boost me, it's not advisable to transport more than one person that far. For one, I don't want to portal into the unknown. For another, I don't want to drain myself when I might have to fight upon arrival or soon after. As I mentioned, my master had access to a permanent portal when he took us to Brazil, but I don't. In saying all that, I think the distance between...Rio de Janeiro and Macapá, you said? Yes, to Macapá should be fine. I'll require some time to rest afterward, as that's just shy of a three-thousand-kilometer distance, but it will cut down on our travel time and expenses."

"Unless you want to portal again, you can rest easily on the boat to Pará. There's only towns and villages along the river," Hugh assured him. "And that sounds splendid, truly. I'm all for saving some time. There's no real rush. My business partner won't send anymore crews in until we have this sorted. This business will likely take a month to settle, at the very least. I do need to stay in Macapá for at least a day to speak with my business partner. I want to be fully up to date before we leave for the mine."

Adrien had taken on jobs that took longer than that, but not by much, and not by preference. If it was anyone other than Hugh Quartermain asking, he wouldn't be as willing to go. But in truth, it sounded like a good challenge, served as an excellent teaching situation for Julian and MacMallin, and got him out of thrice-cursed England for a spell. All of which he needed. If it helped out a friend in the process, well, all the better. "Are we still leaving in seven days?"

"Yes, the plan hasn't changed."

"Excellent. Now, we have some news for you. Both boys are now Danverses."

"You adopted them?" Hugh's blue eyes shot wide with surprise.

"Ah, not me. My cousin George did, in fact. Which makes them my cousins as well, after a fashion." An odd thought, now that he'd voiced it. Not unpleasant, just something to wrap his head about.

Hugh toyed with his glass, eyes thoughtful on the boys. "My congratulations."

Julian and MacMallin beamed at him and chorused thank yous.

Well able to read the worry hidden under the lightly delivered well wishes, Adrien tapped a finger against the tabletop to draw Hugh's attention. "I've not changed my mind, put your worry to rest. But MacMallin's still mine, you know, so of course I had him adopted into my family too."

The tension in Hugh's shoulders relaxed. "Glad to hear it."

"I wouldn't miss the chance to be your apprentice for all the world, Master Hugh." MacMallin gave him a cheeky grin.

Hugh chuckled. "Good. Then we must figure out when to dedicate some of your time to me, to continue your training."

Adrien waved an expansive hand in permission. "By all means."

Shifting, Hugh faced MacMallin directly.

"This trip?" MacMallin asked, tone lilting up hopefully.

"That's my hope. I'll teach you some on the journey, when it doesn't interfere with your other studies," Hugh promised him. "Help speed matters along. Not like there will be much else to do on board the ship for days on end, at any rate."

"And you're certain you'll be able to leave in seven days?" Adrien couldn't help but ask. The man had been so tied in knots that even this luncheon had been rescheduled three different times.

A gleam of determination in his eyes, Hugh's expression

turned sharp. "I promise you, nothing will be able to stop me."

Seven days passed in a whirlwind of activity. Emily took the boys shopping on two separate occasions, then stopped by a third time to kidnap them for tea. Adrien had the feeling she'd finally met two people who would be perfectly frank with her and was reveling in it. Since the boys always came back to the flat all smiles, he didn't even think to protest. He was just happy the boys were gaining more people they could rely on.

The day of departure finally dawned. Adrien arranged for Darby to stay with George and Emily. They were shifting over to the country house, which was the best place for an energetic puppy to be. A crowded cruise ship and a collie would not mix well, and he didn't want to drag her into possible danger in Brazil, either. George's young boys were ecstatic to have a puppy to play with, and Darby willingly went along with them, so he was sure it would all be fine. Well, Julian and MacMallin pouted about not having their dog with them, but they'd survive.

After dropping her off, they went directly to the port. Juggling luggage and two overwhelmed apprentices while crammed into a taxi was not the best experience. The situation did not improve upon arrival. The port was busy, to put it mildly. Theirs was not the only taxi dropping passengers off, and porters snagged their trunks and suitcases from the boot with commendable efficiency. Adrien exited the taxi, nose wrinkling at the overwhelming smell of oil and hot pavement, sea brine mixing in with it in a not entirely pleasant fashion. The din of people talking, heavy objects being shuffled about, and calls to board echoed in his ears. They had another good hour before they set sail. Adrien hated rushing and had deliberately gotten them there a little early.

Adrien had sailed more than once, so he was able to navigate directing the porter to their ship, all while dodging around other passengers. It was keeping track of the boys, who kept getting pushed in the throng, that proved the challenge.

Eventually, they boarded. Hugh had arranged for each of them to have very nice berths on the *Magnava*, one of the newest passenger ships to sail. Adrien's single-space cabin had no real room, of course, but he could stretch out his arms in either direction and not slap his hands against the walls in the process, which was a superior experience to the last time he'd sailed anywhere. With their trunks loaded and the boys safely on board, Adrien had nothing to worry about except perhaps that his friend and employer wouldn't make it to the docks on time.

He stood on deck, safely out of the way of the loading crews, and watched for Hugh. The docks were a hub of activity—people walking quickly either to or from a ship, porters with their luggage going in every conceivable direction, livestock being unloaded with noisy protestation, all mixed in with the bellowed commands of the dock masters. It made for a bedlam of noise and Adrien felt buffeted by it. He couldn't wait for them to be underway, where it would surely prove quieter on the open sea.

Among all those many people moving about below, he finally spied a familiar head of copper hair. He smiled reflexively, relieved Hugh had indeed made it without issue.

"Did you know"—MacMallin drifted up to stand at his shoulder—"that every time you see him, you smile?"

Adrien resisted the urge to smack his head against the banister. Not this business again. "Mac. Do cease and desist."

"You like him," MacMallin insisted, fortunately in a low tone that wouldn't carry farther than two feet. "You find him attractive. I know you do, so why do you always protest?"

Turning, he looked his valet dead in the eye. "Because when a man asks for too much, he destroys what he has."

MacMallin opened his mouth on an instinctive protest.

Adrien overrode him. "Mac, I have a man who is intelligent, kind, and good-natured enough to overlook my terrible reputation and prickly personality. He chooses to be my friend despite the numerous pitfalls. I will not jeopardize that by wishing for more."

"You lose so much because you won't take the risk," MacMallin growled, his tone more rhetorical than accusatory. "I thought Jules was bad, the way he hesitates, but I do think you're worse."

Shaking his head, Adrien let this go. "Go see if your future master needs any help."

The reminder did not put MacMallin onto a different train of thought as Adrien had hoped. Instead, he got a glare. "I'll do that, but I'll tell you this before I go: you're entirely wrong to hesitate. He likes you. He's just not sure of how to reach you." With his piece said, MacMallin marched off, grumbling to himself as he moved.

Adrien couldn't help but glance down at Hugh, still below and in the process of boarding. A small part of him wistfully contemplated what it would be like to have MacMallin be right. But the rest of him quickly shushed it. Adrien knew from very painful experience what would happen if he made an unwelcome overture. He wouldn't be foolish enough to repeat that mistake.

Although, god. Hugh Quartermain would be an extraordinary lover. He was the type to be very, very thorough in whatever he turned his hand to. He was also, by nature, very giving and generous. Lovemaking with him would be a feast of delights, no doubt. Adrien felt chills just thinking about it.

What stretched before him was almost three months of quality time with the man. Adrien both welcomed and cursed it. He thoroughly enjoyed spending time with Hugh. On the other hand, the temptation he felt around that man was practically criminal. Could Adrien, in fact, rein in his instincts before he did something irreversible? Hopefully so, as he did not want to risk his friendship with Hugh. It was so much more important than lust.

Shaking the idea off, he deliberately moved back down to his own quarters. He needed a moment to rearrange his face into pleasant lines before he could meet Hugh.

FIVE

Julian had never really considered what an extended cruise on a ship would entail. Before boarding, he'd been far too focused on their destination to ponder it. What chance would he have had to leisurely sail in his old life, after all? Adrien had been kind enough to explain about sailing and helped Julian and Mac pack, which did help Julian's nerves. Still, actually *being* on the ship was another matter entirely.

First of all, it was much more snug confines than he'd expected. As large as the ship was—and you could fit a small town in here just fine—each of the cabins was quite small. And they were in first class, so Julian could only imagine what kind of shoeboxes the economy cabins were like.

There was also the experience of being out on the open water. The ship didn't move much, but there was still this sense of bobbing along on the sea. Not enough to cause seasickness, thankfully. Whenever he walked the deck, the brisk salt air tingled in his nose, too, but not unpleasantly.

Mac shared a cabin with him, with Hugh's and Adrien's cabins right next door to theirs. It gave him some security, that his protectors were so close. Enough for him to sleep soundly that night despite the unfamiliar environment.

Still, Julian woke up early, earlier than usual, and couldn't sit quietly. He felt too antsy. He didn't wish to wake Mac, though, who was still soundly asleep and curled around him. Neither of them had been able to fall asleep last night until Mac had squeezed in with him, which he'd appreciated. Sometimes it was hard for him to ask Mac to stay close. His brother had never made him feel like a burden; it was Julian's own brain that suggested such. He knew he wasn't a burden to Mac, but sometimes the insidious little voice was too loud. Mac, fortunately, always took the lead when Julian hesitated.

Julian quietly extricated himself, dressed, then grabbed his bag and wand before slipping out. Not knowing where else to go, he headed for the dining hall, where they'd had dinner the night before. Breakfast service was underway, so he put in a request for kippers, boiled eggs, and toast with Earl Grey tea. It came quickly and he tucked in with gusto. Ah, good food. He'd surely gain a stone on this voyage if they kept serving food like this.

Julian was not by any means the only one inside the dining room. Other guests filtered in—couples, families with young children, elderly people, all sorts. Julian, for the most part, ignored them, focusing on the books he'd brought with him. Unlike most his age, who would do anything to get out of studying, Julian relished new knowledge. He loved learning all by itself, but he also loved seeing that proud smile on Adrien's face when Julian did a spell correctly. Julian sometimes lived for that praise.

His reading level was still abysmal, so whenever he had a minute, he'd read. He could comfortably read a storybook now and pushed himself by reading harder and harder books. This one was a beginner's spell book, heavy with illustrations. Adrien had given it to him, saying it would be good reading practice and he could learn many of the basic spells. Two birds, one stone, essentially.

This section was all about healing potions, which surprised Julian, as he'd always thought of potions as more advanced work. But there were a number here, like balms for a burn or minor scrapes. Fascinating, how few ingredients and magic went into making them. No wonder most pharmacies carried them. They were cheap and easy to make—

On the other side of the open dining room, a cry of alarm went up, very quickly followed by a muted crashing sound as glass broke. Startled, Julian looked up and around, ascertaining the source of the noise. Ah, there, a little girl stood in front of a tray, a waiter next to her appearing dismayed and a middle-aged woman behind her, seeming more annoyed than anything.

"This is why I told you not to rush around," the woman said to the child, exasperated. "Now look at you. There's no possible way to get those stains out of your dress."

Julian appraised the child and felt his heart go out to her as he saw the obvious purple blotch—likely from a juice the waiter had been carrying—soaking through the front of her white dress. She couldn't be more than eight or nine, and this public scolding made an already embarrassing situation that much worse. She stared at the carpeted floor, red all the way up to her ears, tears streaming down her cheeks.

Julian felt compelled up to his feet. He had no doubt that if Adrien or Hugh had been here, they would render assistance. It was what a gentleman would do, and what he should do.

He hurried in that direction, weaving expertly around the dining tables, already drawing his platinum wand from his coat pocket. "I say, may I be of assistance?"

The trio looked at him, the little girl peeking up through her blonde lashes. The woman appeared flustered, staring at the wand in some confusion but with an air of enlightenment. Most sorcerers used a wand as a focusing tool and channel. Adrien didn't, but he was one of those who truly *understood* magic and because of that rarely needed a wand. Julian kept his on him as training wheels. It helped while he figured out how magic and spells worked.

Julian gave the mother his best street smile, the one that always charmed and put people at ease. "Julian Danvers, at your assistance."

"Danvers. As in Adrien Danvers, the famous sorcerer?"

"I'm his apprentice, madam." He took her hand and bowed over it, still maintaining the smile. "I can clean this up without much trouble."

She glanced between the mess on the floor and the girl's stained white dress, grimacing. "If you'd be so kind."

"Certainly."

Julian had developed a newfound appreciation for repair and cleaning spells since becoming an apprentice. Mostly because he seemed to need them at every turn, as not much about learning magic went right on the first try. He was quite confident in these spells and used them without hesitation.

First, the little girl's dress—Julian didn't want to appear to think her less important than the mess on the floor. He aimed the wand and spoke the spell clearly, enunciating each syllable. In seconds, the purple stain dried up and vanished as if it had never been. Then he pointed to the broken pottery and glass on the floor, cleaning first the food and drink stains from the carpet before repairing the broken dishes. The waiter promptly stooped and scooped the dishes up, replacing them on the tray.

He gave a nod to Julian. "My thanks, sir. The manager can

reward you—"

Julian lifted a hand to stay the offer. "While appreciated, it's not necessary. I could hardly leave a damsel in distress."

The waiter was an older gentleman, and he gave Julian an approving smile. "Very good, sir."

Now, only one thing left to do. Julian drew his handkerchief from a pocket and used it to dab at those round cheeks, erasing signs of tears. The little girl didn't cry any longer but stared at him with a sort of dazed confusion, big blue eyes blinking up at him.

"Are you hurt at all?" he asked gently.

She shook her head no, still staring as if not sure what to make of him. "Are you a sorcerer?"

"One in training, yes."

"Do you fight dragons?"

"Amelia." The woman sighed, as if done with the child already. "Shouldn't you say thank you first?"

"Thank you." Amelia then promptly repeated, "Do you fight dragons?"

"I've not yet fought a dragon," he said, amused at her persistence. "But I have assisted in fighting sea serpents. Does that count?"

Her eyes went wide with wonder. "Were they very big?"

"Huge. As large as a house. And mean." Sensing that she might be the type to love all things fantastical, he leaned in and whispered, "My master is a grand sorcerer, and he and Sir Hugh Quartermain fought side by side to subdue it. It was quite the fight."

Bingo. Her eyes sparkled like he'd told her the most amazing tale. "A knight and a sorcerer? It's just like my storybook!"

Ah-ha. No wonder she was fixated on this idea. "Those kinds of tales do happen in real life as well. Now, may I assist you to your table?"

She took his hand, letting him escort her back to her seat, but peppered him with questions as they went. Much to the dismay of whom Julian assumed was her mother.

"If a sea serpent attacks the ship, will your master fight it, too?"

"Of course. Actually, the knight is with us on this trip, so he'll fight it as well."

"What about a dragon?"

"Amelia." Her mother groaned, a hand to her head. "I'll murder your father for giving you that storybook. Do stop badgering the young man. He has better things to do than stand here and answer all your questions."

He did, but he was amused enough to play along for a moment more. "I assure you, Miss Amelia, whatever attacks the boat won't live for long. You're safe as houses here."

That seemed to satisfy her. Perhaps reassure her, as she relaxed into her seat. "If I see a dragon or a sea serpent, I'll tell you."

"I would appreciate that." He winked at her, gave the mother an incline of his head, and went back to his table to collect his books. He was done with breakfast, and it seemed best to change locations before Amelia thought of any more questions. A lounge chair on the upper deck was just the thing. He could get some fresh air and continue studying at the same time.

Before he could leave the dining area, a man in a dark suit rushed up to him, speed walking in such a way that he resembled a penguin. An uncharitable thought, but true nonetheless.

"Mister Danvers?" he asked, puffing to a stop.

It was very odd to be addressed so. In fact, he was the first to ever address Julian as a mister. It gave Julian a start. A pleasant one.

"Yes, sir. May I help you?"

"I'm Harvey, the manager over the dining area. I'm told you did us a great service and would like to thank you."

Oh dear, seemed he got to do this song and dance again. "Think nothing of it, sir. I was happy to help."

"I don't think you appreciate just how much help that was. We lost two crates of plates due to an accident while loading, so we're short on them. We really cannot afford any more loss."

Julian blinked at him. "Good heavens, *two* crates?"

Harvey gave a hangdog slump. "I wish I was jesting. We even had cushioning spells on them, but, well…"

"They didn't do the job." Julian thought on it, then decided, why not? It would be good practice. "Do you still have the crates?"

Harvey straightened slowly, hope dawning over his features. "We do. I was set to throw them overboard today, but if you'd be willing to mend them…?"

"Lead the way."

Harvey beamed at him, turning sideways to gesture toward the kitchen door. "This way. I say, capital good luck having a sorcerer on board."

Yes, for Harvey it certainly was. "I'm an apprentice, in fact. My master is taking me along on a job to Brazil."

"Is that right? Well, all the better. Here, come through here."

He pushed through a swinging white door, leading Julian through the kitchen. It was organized chaos back here, with men and women all occupied with chopping things or cooking dishes on the stove. Harvey ducked around them with practiced ease, leaving Julian scurrying to keep up.

In the very back of the room was a row of shelves and two large sinks sitting side by side. On the far side of the sinks, stacked in a corner, were the crates in question. They couldn't be anything else—the crates looked like they'd survived a war and barely lived to tell the tale. It was a wonder they were holding together at all.

Julian couldn't begin to estimate how many plates were in those crates. The crates themselves were large enough for him to squeeze into, but that told him nothing. "How many plates are there inside?"

"Approximately one hundred in each." Harvey was back to looking uncertain. "Um, I don't know if you can fix all two hundred in one go, but whatever you can do, I'd be thankful."

"I think I can do most of them, but I might have to come back tomorrow and finish up." Julian honestly didn't know. He'd never done a great deal of spell work like this all in one go. Normally, he'd try a spell, perhaps repeat it a dozen times, and then call it done. Adrien told him on a regular basis that he was powerful—and Julian had no reason to doubt his master—he just didn't know how much he could feasibly do all at once.

"Is it possible to get the lid off? Rather hard to mend when I can't see what I'm doing."

"Oh, of course, of course!" Harvey turned and gestured to someone else. "Joe, come help with this."

Joe, a beefy man who could easily be a heavyweight boxer, promptly came over.

"This is a young sorcerer," Harvey explained. "Said he could mend the plates but needs the lid off."

"Right on." Joe flashed Julian a smile. "That'll make things much easier round here. Gimme two shakes."

Joe's muscles were not for show. He had the top of the crate off in a second flat, despite not using any kind of crowbar. The nails didn't stand a chance, though they did squeal in protest as the lid was taken off—a rather obnoxious sound.

With the lid off, Julian could see the mess inside. It looked... bad. All the plates had been smashed almost beyond recognition, just shards sitting on top of shards. Julian stared inside, perplexed. "Did a boulder fall on this or something?"

Harvey sighed, aggravated all over again. "Damn crane operator lost control of them, slammed them right against the pier, then apparently decided they were fine without checking and loaded them anyway. I radioed back to port the second I discovered the crates and gave them an earful, I did. Doesn't help us with this situation, though."

Ah. That would explain this, all right. "No cushioning spell could withstand an impact such as that. It's not rated for that kind of protection. But either way, I think I can fix this. Where do you want the mended plates to go?"

"The sink, if you would."

They did have packing dust all over them and probably could stand a wash before being put to use. Julian shrugged, lifted his wand, and once again spoke the mending spell. This time, he expanded the area to encompass the whole crate. Somewhat to his surprise, they all came together neatly, without any strain on his part. Huh. Well, perhaps he was underestimating himself.

Pleased at his success, he levitated the plates over to the sink, and they settled with a small clatter in the large basin.

"Did he just fix the plates?" a woman demanded, heading toward them with her not-inconsiderable figure. "Praise be, he did! Jolly good show there, young man. I'm Matilda Craig, head chef upon this vessel."

Julian took the hand she extended, giving a bow over it, which flustered her for some reason. "Chef, a pleasure. I'm Julian Danvers, apprentice to Adrien Danvers."

"Oh! I heard he was on board. No idea an apprentice was with him." Her smile went ear to ear, revealing a gap between two of her front teeth. "You're doing good work here, Apprentice Danvers. Life saving for us. All last night we had to wash dishes the second they hit the kitchen, then turn around and use them again the next second. I don't mind telling you, that caused chaos in here all through dinner, and none of us wanted a repeat."

Ouch. That would be brutal, to keep up that kind of pace. "I'm happy to help, Chef."

"You won't be charged for a single meal while you're on this ship," Chef Craig swore. "That's my reward for you. Can you do the other crate?"

"I can." Having just done one, he was sure of it. "Joe, if you'd be so kind as to shift this busted crate out of the way?"

Joe was already on it, all too happy to assist. With the wood moved and the top off the second crate, Julian was able to see the shards and use the mending spell again. Huh, still no real strain. He'd have to ask Adrien about this. Was there some sort of test Julian could do to tell him what his magical limits were?

In any case, not the moment for it. Harvey inspected the plates, one at a time, beaming. "Not even a chip! Good work, Apprentice. You've saved us sanity and a lot of money. I'll tell your master about this later. I'm sure he'll be pleased."

"He likely will." Julian smiled at the thought. "Is there anything else I can assist you with?"

"Bless you, not a thing." Chef Craig took him by the arm, escorting him back out, a bounce in her step. "And you let me know if you want something special. The kitchen is at your beck and call now."

He wouldn't, as that would cause trouble for the kitchen, but he appreciated the offer. "Everything I've had so far is delicious. I'll take whatever you make."

"Aren't you a smooth one?" Chef Craig cackled as she took him through the swinging doors. "The ladies are going to eat you up when you come of age."

Hopefully not. He'd much prefer a handsome gentleman. "Sounds terrifying."

She cackled again, then gave him a pat on the shoulder. "Give it time, lad, give it time. I'm back to the breakfast rush, but cheers."

Julian took himself out of the dining room, pleased with the way this morning had gone. If he kept helping people like that, would he gain a reputation? Julian hoped so. Adrien Danvers left very big shoes to fill, and Julian honestly wasn't sure if he was up to the task. All he could do was try.

Which meant back to studying. He found an empty lounge chair under the portico, shaded from the morning sun, but still with that lovely ocean breeze flowing over him. He settled in, found his page, and became utterly absorbed.

He paused as he read, carefully sounding out the words he didn't know, mouth moving almost silently.

"Can you read it all, lad?" asked a voice he recognized from over his shoulder.

Julian craned his neck around and up to look at Hugh Quartermain. "For the most part, sir. And good morning."

"Good morning. Your reading skills are catching up quickly. That's a more advanced book than the last one I saw you reading."

Julian beamed at him, pleased at the praise. "I read every chance I get."

"Best way to improve," Hugh said with a nod. "Can I interest you in putting the book aside for a moment? Nothing's due to start for a while yet and I feel we should take advantage. Do you know how to play whist?"

Intrigued, Julian stood up from his lounger and shook his head. "No, sir."

Hugh put a hand on his shoulder. "That won't do, lad. Won't do at all. It's a popular game among the upper crust. They play it often after dinner. You're a proper Danvers now. Best you know how to play."

Julian was quite amenable to this, and since Mac hadn't emerged from their shared cabin yet and Adrien was nowhere to be seen, he didn't mind passing some time with Hugh. He followed the man's lead into an adjoining room, which was set up for evening entertainment and games. Playing on the deck was sure to end poorly. The wind would no doubt take off with the cards. Julian set his books aside and sat at the round table with its snowy white tablecloth, bending his attention to the rules as Hugh explained them. There was a deck of cards on each table, and he saw what Hugh meant about card games being popular.

With the rules explained, Hugh dealt them both a hand. Julian struggled to remember everything as he carefully chose his strategy, picking his cards to play to the trick. The game was supposed to be played with four people, two each in partnership, but for a rough and ready version they were making do with two.

As he slowly got the hang of which card to play and the strategies involved, it gave him the freedom to breathe a little. Julian decided to prod and see if Hugh had changed his mind about courting Adrien. "We had dinner with my new cousins last week."

"Did you? Which cousins?"

"George and Emily Danvers."

"The ones who adopted you?"

"The same, sir. They're quite splendid."

"I've met Lord Danvers socially a time or two." Hugh drew a card and frowned at his hand. "An overall good chap was my impression of him. He had a keen interest in the mechanics of factories, said he wanted to invest in a few. We had quite the conversation about it during one of those interminable soirees. Never did follow up with him to see if he wanted to invest in one of mine."

"I think he does. He asked quite a few questions of Mac when we had dinner with them, wanting to know all about your new factory."

"Did he?" Hugh asked, expression ruminative. "I'll look him up when we get home again, then. I take it that you're settling in well with your new relatives?"

"Oh yes, rather," Julian said with relish. "Emily is very kind. She's taken us shopping for new clothes and arranged a tutor for us once we return to London. Even took us out to tea just because. She's *full* of questions and is delighted we don't mince words around her."

Hugh snorted in amusement. "Lord, I wish I could listen in on one of those conversations. They're sure to be a doozy."

"I did try to be delicate the first time," Julian said in defense, then paused as he frowned at his hand. Absolutely nothing would suit to continue the trick. He went with the next best option. "She told me very firmly that if she wanted to have that sort of picked-over conversation, she'd be speaking to her husband. Then Mac said something perfectly scandalous and she clapped, she was so pleased, and immediately asked another question. I reckoned she really wanted the blunt truth and haven't tried to be delicate with her since."

Hugh gave him a sardonic look. "That, and you're having fun trying to shock her."

Julian grinned unrepentantly. "And that. Although, to be fair, she started it. She and Cousin George have assured Master that he and his lover will be very welcome at any time. Master's even under orders to bring his lover with him during holidays."

Hugh stilled, staring at Julian as if trying to discern his true intentions. "Is that right?"

"Left Master quite befuddled," Julian said innocently, daring only a peek up from his cards. "But happy, too, I think. Master's expression was priceless, though. Pity you missed it."

"Yes, I'm sorry I did too." Hugh frowned at his hand, but Julian had a feeling it wasn't the cards at fault.

"How goes that front?" Julian might as well ask. Perhaps he could give some advice.

Hugh sighed, setting the cards down for a moment. "It's difficult. Adrien has his guard up so thoroughly, it's hard to know how to approach him."

"He's been hurt too many times." Julian knew this for a fact. "Miss Stacey has told us a few stories, and they're rather upsetting. He's very anxious, too, about losing his friendship with you by asking for more."

Hugh's expression grew very dark indeed, almost murderous. "I'll strangle whoever made him feel less than. He shouldn't be so cautious. I've admitted to him that I have friends and family from all walks of life and that he needn't be so reserved with me. It did seem to have some good effect, but I'm not sure if he believed it."

"He did. It's why he told you as much as he did. But he really adores you, Sir Hugh. He just doesn't want to risk you."

Hugh sighed, head sinking into one hand. "I'm glad to hear it but aggravated at the same time. I'll find a way to get through to him. Thanks for telling me, Julian."

Julian was secretly relieved Hugh didn't seem at all inclined to stop his pursuit. "If you want a hint...?"

Hugh looked up, brows rising. "I like hints."

"Touch seems to work very well with him. He tenses at first, as if unused to it, but he always relaxes when we seek comfort from him."

"Touch, eh?" Hugh absorbed this information, nodding slowly. "Touch. All right, that I can do."

Whatever else Julian might have said was lost as Adrien and Mac joined them at the card table. "There you are," Adrien said as he came to stand next to the table. "What's this, then? Whist?"

"Thought he'd best know how to play," Hugh said, folding his cards together temporarily to address Adrien. "You know how cruises go, everyone's always playing cards or sharing gossip."

"And getting drunk," Adrien agreed with a snort. "Yes, rather. Hard to teach him all the strategies with only two players, though. Come, Mac, sit for a spell. Best you learn this too. How about masters and apprentices partner up and play against each other?"

For Mac's sake, Hugh explained the rules again even as Adrien collected all the cards and shuffled them. Julian had never seen his master with a playing deck in hand until this moment. It was rather educational. Adrien shuffled them together back and forth, bridges and fans, like a professional gambler. Miss Stacey had once warned Julian and Mac that Adrien was the absolute worst at cards. He now rather understood what she'd meant.

Julian wasn't the only one to take notice, as Hugh broke off to frown at him. "I say, Adrien. How good are you at cards?"

"Decent." Adrien innocently batted his lashes.

"Uh-huh." Mac stared at Adrien with clear distrust. "I don't believe that."

"That's because you have good common sense, lad," Hugh muttered. "All right, Adrien, hand the deck over."

"No one ever trusts me with a deck," Adrien grumbled cheerfully.

Julian glanced at his master from the corner of his eye. He wondered at this strange mood of his master's. Adrien was normally quite straitlaced, somber and uptight. His smiles came rarely, his laughter even more so. And yet he was in a fine humor now, a smile permanently curving his mouth upward. Was it the notion that he'd be with Hugh for an extended period of time? Or that he was leaving England behind? It could be either, or even both.

Julian wasn't the only one who picked up on it. Hugh asked casually, "Are you excited to be on your way to Brazil, Adrien?"

"That and leaving England altogether. As I've mentioned before, it's not my favorite country." Adrien frowned at his hand and rearranged his cards.

Hugh lifted an eyebrow in curiosity. "You mentioned before you're staying till the boys are more comfortable in their studies, correct?"

"Mm. I do have business in England on a regular basis. But yes, right now it's these two keeping me there, but I hope to be back in Bangkok soon. Really, the only reason I keep the flat is for when I have a job or when Prince Henry calls for me." Adrien made a sour face. "He unfortunately does that rather often. Never mind that he's got his own sorcerer."

"I've met the prince regent's sorcerer a time or two. I can't say I came away with a good impression of her," Hugh said levelly.

Adrien snorted. "Nor I. Julian, you fortunately missed meeting her when we were called in by Prince Henry for Sebastian's case. But you'll soon see what we mean. Marianne Kent is better connected than anyone short of the royal family, but she has a very brute force approach to solving problems."

Hearing them speak of a highly positioned sorcerer in such a manner didn't sound quite right to Julian. Any sorcerer appointed as the official sorcerer to a royal person was formidable in their own right. They had to be, to fulfill the duties given to them. "But... she must be good."

"Oh, she's quite good. I'm not saying otherwise. I just know sorcerers who are far better. Everyone does, and it grates on Kent. She knows very well she shouldn't have the position. That she only has it because of her connections. Prince Henry doesn't use her often. Barely at all, in fact. Every time he calls for me to do some task for him, it enrages her even further. It also demeans her standing that Prince Henry obviously doesn't trust her in such a position and chooses to call someone else in."

That sounded potentially troublesome to Julian. "But you don't like Prince Henry. If you don't like him, and you know by going you'll make an enemy of his sorcerer, then why attend him?"

"Two reasons, really." Adrien laid out a pair of cards and picked up the next, gesturing for Hugh to take his turn. "One, he pays very, very well. Two, it increasingly boosts my own reputation. It's the best sort of advertisement possible, to have a prince call for you. I don't like Prince Henry, but I don't absolutely hate him. While I would rather not, I can stomach briefly working for him. Proving that Kent is incapable of serving in her position is an added bonus."

Hugh snorted and laid down a rather clever trick that Jules promptly made mental note of. "Have you not considered that Prince Henry is slowly luring you in?"

Startled, Adrien jerked his head up to stare at Hugh. "Luring me in?"

"To become the prince regent's sorcerer, to take Sorceress

Kent's position," Hugh elaborated patiently. "If he's routinely calling for you, then—"

"Hugh, don't be obtuse. The prince regent would rather stab himself in the eye with an ice pick than have me constantly underfoot. He uses me to both get the job done well and to further antagonize a woman he severely dislikes but is unfortunately saddled with. I'm a pawn in a power game he's playing, nothing more."

Julian didn't for one second believe that. Adrien didn't understand, sometimes, just how much people respected his immense ability. Julian suspected Prince Henry didn't really dislike his master at all, but instead was giving tit for tat whenever they clashed. Adrien might be too close to the situation to see it for what it was.

From his expression, Hugh shared the opinion but let it go with a shrug. "We'll be on the ship for a good twenty days. Have you thought of a tutoring schedule yet?"

"I rather thought I could teach the boys reading and maths in the morning, then after lunch, we could divide and conquer. Each take our own apprentice, I mean."

Hugh nodded amenably. "Sound enough plan, I think. In fact, Mac, I have something of a project that I brought along with me. Fellow over in America invented a self-developing camera. No darkroom required. I bought one. Let's take it apart, shall we, see if we can't reverse engineer it. I want to see if it's possible to manufacture this or not."

Mac shone with eagerness. "Yes, sir. If you can, then will you buy the patent for it?"

"I certainly will. Best to make sure it's feasible first, though, before I invest anything in it."

Julian listened to this conversation with growing interest. Was there anything in the world that didn't catch Hugh Quartermain's attention? Apparently not. And just how intelligent was the man, that he could take something apart and figure it out from there? Julian possessed no doubt that he could do so, either. He felt a little envious. Would he himself ever reach an age where he had that sort of confidence?

"Are you talking or playing?" Adrien asked in a teasing voice.

Making a face, Mac focused on his cards long enough to be able to lay something down. Julian, in turn, had to figure out what to play. From the corner of his eye, he watched his brother animatedly discuss the camera with his new master, and he felt another wave of intense gratitude to his own master. Thank god Adrien Danvers had been the one to discover him on that cold, brutal night so many months ago. If anyone else had found him, Julian might not have this scene, this happiness.

He'd not trade it for anything in the world.

Six

Hugh's cabin had a small sitting area off to one side, a true luxury on a ship of any size. He'd only dreamed of such wealth when he was a youngster, but now, he relished comfort. Not to mention room to spread out in. If he'd attempted to go three full weeks without tinkering, he'd have been a candidate for Bedlam soon enough.

Besides, his inventions demanded a certain amount of caution and secrecy. It wasn't something he could do out in the common area of the ship.

The sitting area wasn't large by any stretch of the imagination. It boasted a single table, barely enough to seat two, and two simple wooden chairs with basic cushions. The portholes on the wall gave adequate light to work by. Hugh had certainly worked in worse conditions. Having spent a few days going over schematic examples and familiarizing MacMallin with both common and uncommon terminology in the field, Hugh decided he could reward his apprentice's hard work by letting him tinker. A simple enough arrangement, at least, and that was all Hugh wanted to do today.

Hugh set the camera down on the table, a stack of paper and two drafting pencils ready and waiting off to the side. He looked at his new apprentice and was amused to find MacMallin had somehow gained a good two inches since the Isle of Man. There was barely half a head of difference now between them.

MacMallin glowed with excitement, his eyes fixed on the camera. It was a suitable beginner's project for the lad. Taking something apart and learning how to keep track of the pieces was a good habit to form from the very beginning.

"Now, remember what I said last time. The trick is to keep accurate notes of what you're doing and to not put the pieces in a special spot. You always lose them if you do. So after you dismantle something, remember to make note of it."

Nodding, MacMallin pointed eagerly toward the awaiting screwdriver. "Can I start?"

"Certainly. Have at it."

He promptly did so, fitting the screwdriver into the head of the screw and turning it.

Leaning back in his chair, Hugh looked at his all-too-serious apprentice and couldn't resist the urge to pull his leg a mite. "Now, Mac, two things you need to keep in mind with machines. First thing is, if it abruptly stops working, odds are that some dirt has gotten in where it isn't supposed to. If you take it apart, clean everything, and put it back together, it'll often work."

MacMallin stopped unscrewing long enough to shoot him a questioning lift of an eyebrow. "Is that so?"

"Machines are more finicky than you'd think. Now, second thing you must be aware of is that machines run on smoke."

His apprentice stopped dead, brows furrowing in confusion. "What? Smoke?"

"Indeed. You've seen a machine when it stops working, how it'll let out a huge cloud of smoke before it shuts down? That's the smoke it's running on. If it escapes, well, it breaks." Hugh fought to keep his face straight.

Proving that he had a good ear for nonsense, MacMallin demanded suspiciously, "Are you joshing me, sir?"

Hugh's facial muscles couldn't hold it in anymore and he grinned mischievously. "Only a little. It's an old engineer's joke that my master told to me. Something of a running joke in the industry. Whenever something breaks, we always blame it first on the smoke escaping."

"But why do machines usually break, sir?"

"Because they want to and they can. Be grateful for that, as it validates the existence of us engineers."

MacMallin worked at getting the casing of the camera off, then took a diligent note that looked more illustration than words, which was acceptable. Hugh had done this so many times that he could observe and retain it all. This exercise was more for MacMallin's benefit than anything. If illustrations helped him, then illustrations it would be.

"Sir, you can be honest with me," MacMallin said, his eyes never leaving the camera. "You took me on to get a step closer to

Master Adrien."

Hugh looked at this bright, earnest child and felt his heart break a little at the insecurity rolling off him in waves. "Mac, I'll honestly say that I don't mind that benefit, but that's not why. I looked at you and I saw a younger version of myself."

MacMallin's head snapped up and around, golden eyes wide. "You?"

"Indeed. The same curiosity, the same drive to understand, the same twitching hands dying to tinker. You've the mind for it, Mac. I've seen you work, seen that clever mind analyzing and coming up with solutions. I can see the potential in you clearly. Someone just had to give you a chance." Hugh phrased the next part carefully. "And we're a bit similar in other ways, too. You do know that I'm the bastard son of an earl?"

The teenager's jaw dropped as he spluttered. "Cor, blimey!"

Hugh ignored the street slang, although it amused him. "Hadn't heard that, eh? Indeed, lad, the only reason why I was apprenticed was that my paternal grandmother took pity on me and paid the apprenticeship fees. I've never let the start of my life define who I could become. I've never let anyone else define me by that, either. Adrien firmly wants a good future for you, and I'm inclined to help him with that. Do I find it attractive that Adrien Danvers has moved the world to give you and Julian a better future? Of course, lad, I'm not blind. Will I take advantage of the connection? Of course, as I'm not stupid. Did I take you as an apprentice for those two reasons? Of course not, I'm not foolish. You will be my successor. You damn well better be up to the task."

MacMallin's jaw was still dangling. Pointing to himself, he croaked, "Me? Succeed you?"

"I've no children and no other apprentices," Hugh said, still amused. "Who the devil is supposed to get it all when I die, then? Of course you."

MacMallin went sideways in the chair, making it skitter and rattle on the floor, looking completely overwhelmed. Hugh charitably gave him a minute, as MacMallin needed one to absorb this.

"You trust me with it," MacMallin whispered, still stunned. "You trust me with it all?"

British men didn't normally display much physical affection, but Hugh was not of that kind of stock. He didn't know how

MacMallin felt about it, but in this case, the lad looked sorely in need of a hug. Hugh gathered him into his side and hugged him tight for a moment before releasing him. "You'll be fine. I've got a good eye for quality. It's not failed me yet. Unless you don't wish to have all this responsibility?"

Shaking his head adamantly, MacMallin scrambled, words falling on top of each other. "No, that's not it. Of course it's...I'll work to earn it, sir."

"That's the spirit. Let's start with figuring out if that camera actually works and is worth the investment."

MacMallin seemed glad to have a focus and he returned to the task, a breathtaking smile still lingering over his face. He worked for several minutes, examining the best way to take the lens off, before he stopped and whispered shyly to Hugh, "I hope he falls in love with you, sir. I hope you can catch his heart. He needs someone like you."

Now that was an interesting statement. "In what way?"

"Someone who will give him a hug when he needs it."

That statement validated something Hugh had instinctively felt. Adrien Danvers sometimes reacted like a man starved for genuine affection. Especially at their first acquaintance, Hugh had garnered that impression. Adrien had improved some since—no doubt the addition of his cousins had helped ease the need—but something of it still lingered in him, that craving. Hugh suspected part of the reason why Adrien had so readily taken in both Julian and MacMallin was because he saw two kindred souls who also needed love and attention. By giving them affection, he hoped to earn some in return.

MacMallin, street-raised as he was, had all the necessary instincts to see the situation as it stood. If even he felt that way about Adrien, then Hugh's impression must be correct. For that matter, Julian had said the same. With both of them providing validation, he'd be wise to move on it.

He'd not planned to do this quite so soon, but perhaps the timing was right for it.

"I hope so, too. Mac, let me show you something." Hugh stood and fetched the carved wooden box from the side table, opening it as he turned to display the cuff inside. He'd forged and made it himself, the stone flat and sparkling like captured moonlight in the black leather of the cuff. It was some of the mithril from his caves—the mithril Adrien had nearly died protecting. "I made this for him. Do you think he'll like it?"

MacMallin lifted a hand, tracing the edging of the neatly sewn leather with wonder. "Sir, it's exquisite. That's mithril, isn't it?"

"Yes, quite. I thought it best to give him something he can keep on him that will boost his power."

"He'll be over the moon with it."

"I'll show you how to craft it, if you wish to create one for Julian, too."

MacMallin nodded eagerly before he could finish the sentence. "Yes, sir, truly. Jules needs it just as much."

"I quite agree. To that end…" Hugh went and fetched the small wooden case he'd shoved under his bed for safekeeping. Pulling it out, he handed it to MacMallin. "Your tools, young apprentice."

"Tools?" MacMallin accepted the polished dark wood case with both hands, then set it down on an empty section of the table to open it up. The top two trays opened to either side as he lifted the lid, displaying a neat selection of wires, screwdrivers, clamps, a hammer, wrenches, and other paraphernalia Hugh had found to be helpful over the years. MacMallin stared at it, lost of words.

"You'll find a good choice of tools in there, but you might add or take things out of it as time goes on. This is just what's in my toolbox, and what I've found handy to keep on me."

MacMallin lunged out of his chair and hugged Hugh hard around the waist. The impact was enough to make Hugh rock on his heels and he gave an *oomph*, then a gentle chuckle as he hugged MacMallin firmly back. "You're welcome."

"It's the best present ever, sir. I'll cherish it."

"Good. Use it, too. Tools need to be used."

MacMallin grinned up at him. "I will. Camera first. Then something for Julian?"

"Aye. I brought an assortment of different shapes of leathers and clasps. We'll see what we can design for him."

MacMallin pulled back, giving him a scrutinizing study that suggested he was trying to see right to the back of Hugh's skull. Then he said bluntly, "I've noticed you're being more hands-on with Master Adrien. Keep at it, sir. I can see it chipping away at his defenses."

A delighted smile burst over Hugh's face. "Is it? He's very hard for me to read sometimes. Thanks, lad, that bolsters my nerve."

"Thought it would, sir. Jules and I will try to give you moments alone."

"That'll be deucedly helpful. The man's hard to catch one on one."

"That I know, sir." MacMallin went back to his toolbox before drawing up short once more. "But, sir, what if I put this camera back together wrong?"

"Then we take it apart once more and try again." Hugh kept his tone patient. He remembered well what it was like to be the apprentice, the one afraid of failure. It would be best to drum that fear out of MacMallin now, if he could. "No harm in that, lad. We engineers rarely get it right on the first try. 'Try, try again' is the motto we live and breathe by. Often, on the second go round, we think of a way to do it better."

The tension in MacMallin subsided. "Hadn't thought of it that way, sir. But really? You have to redo things all the time?"

"All the time." Hugh sighed, only partially exaggerating the mannerism.

"Worst story," MacMallin said immediately, a wicked glint in his eye.

He was no doubt trying to pull Hugh's leg, but truthfully, Hugh was delighted he felt comfortable enough to do so. Hugh wasn't the least put off by this demand. Chuckling low in his chest, he settled back in the chair, legs crossed. "What springs to mind is a very misspent day in my youth, when I was too young to know better but old enough to think I did. It all started when I found a busted radio thrown out back of the shop..."

Seven

It was five days into the voyage and Adrien was pleased it was going so well. Neither boy had become seasick (his worst fear), and Julian had done the kitchen staff a good turn, so they were very friendly with him. Really, all of it was good practice for Julian, not only in terms of practicing magic but also in dealing with clients. It had noticeably improved his confidence as well. As a master, Adrien couldn't be prouder.

Adrien was in the midst of dressing for dinner—this time without MacMallin's help—his hands busy with his tie, when there was a knock at the door. He'd told MacMallin to see to himself and Julian, to not mind him, but apparently the boy couldn't help himself. Rolling his eyes, he called out, "Enter!"

The door clacked open behind him. "I hope I'm not intruding."

Eh? Startled, Adrien turned sharply about, not expecting Hugh. It took him a moment to find his tongue. "Not at all. Do you need something?"

"I wanted to find a private moment to give you something."

He looked quite dashing in his dark navy suit, Adrien couldn't help but notice. The blue was a perfect complement to his copper hair and was cut in such a fashion that it highlighted his strong build. Adrien swallowed hard and did his utmost to not ogle.

It proved difficult.

Not to mention, having a man of Hugh's size in the close confines of the cabin felt...intense. Not stifling, but almost overwhelming in a way. This close, Adrien could smell the man's cologne invading his nose. Yearning hit him in the pit of his stomach.

An embarrassing amount of time later, Hugh's words penetrated and Adrien questioned them. "Give me something? I've done nothing to warrant a gift."

Hugh approached with a steady tread, a smile lifting the

corners of the man's eyes. He slipped an item from his pocket, a small carved wooden box, which he displayed on a palm as he opened it. "I hope you don't mind the handmade quality of it, but I wanted to make this for you myself."

What in the wide green world could he possibly have made…?

The final fold of fabric pulled away, revealing the most beautifully tooled leather cuff Adrien had ever laid eyes upon. It had been neatly stitched on the sides, the pattern of vines like filigree around the stone set in the middle of it. The mithril had been shaped into a flat disk, oval in shape, and carefully encased in the black leather.

"It's beautiful," Adrien breathed, taken aback by the cuff. He'd never in his life been given anything like it. Hugh had given him access to an excess of mithril after the sea serpent case, and Adrien always kept at least an ingot in his work bag, but this was different. More personal. Never mind the practicality of it—and having a large amount of mithril like this on his person would be quite the boon—the gift had obviously taken time to make. Time a busy man like Hugh Quartermain didn't have.

He valued Adrien enough to make him this?

"You like it, I can see it from your expression. Good. Let me put it on for you."

Adrien allowed Hugh to push his sleeve up. He then put the cuff on with deft fingers, the metal clasp clicking into place in a perfect fit. A suspiciously perfect fit.

"How did you know my measurements?"

Hugh shrugged as if this was nothing at all. "I measured your wrist while you were still recuperating after the fight with the serpent."

Oh. Of course, he would have had ample time to do so. "Is this in return for the serpent, then? Or for saving your life in the caves?"

"Not at all, although I admit that the fight in the caves sparked the idea." Hugh leaned in a little, eyes warm with affection. "This is because you are dear to me, Adrien, and I wanted to give you something. Nothing less."

This man was bad for Adrien's heart. It was thumping so hard he could feel it beating against his ribs. Hugh was just too gentle of a soul, too kind, too generous. He'd give Adrien all the wrong ideas if he kept doing sweet, thoughtful things like this.

Afraid his eyes would give him away, Adrien looked down at the cuff, a finger tracing the design. "You are incredibly skilled. It's beautiful, thank you."

"I'm glad you like it. I hope it will help protect you, the next time you're up to your neck in some trouble."

"I'm sure it will. Power boosts at desperate moments are always a welcome boon."

Like it was the most natural thing in the world, those square, blunt-tipped fingers rose to the necktie Adrien had abandoned and picked it up. Adrien startled, lifting a hand to stop him.

"I can manage—"

"Hush," Hugh chided gently. "Let me."

Adrien did because he didn't know how to gracefully stop the man. Still, every brush of those warm fingers against his chest sent sparks of delight along Adrien's skin, like Hugh was tapping him just so in order to leave light behind. It made Adrien irrationally hungry for more contact—for a stronger brush of his hand against Adrien's chest. For a simple cloth barrier to not separate them. Hugh had become much more tactile recently and Adrien didn't understand why. It was little things, like him putting a hand against the small of Adrien's back to usher him through a crowd, or playful nudges against his shoulder when Hugh was in high spirits. Was this how the man acted when he became close friends with someone? Or...really, Adrien couldn't think of another reason. He was absolutely confuddled by the behavior, as it made no sense, but the tingles along his skin had him almost leaning into the touch.

Adrien was about to come out of his skin and all the man was doing was tying his necktie.

Maybe his apprentices had a point about him needing a good bout of sex.

Perhaps because he sensed Adrien's nerves, Hugh said in a casual tone, "I've meant to ask, is it only Thai you speak?"

Adrien gave himself a mental shake and focused on the conversation. "Uh, no. I'm also fluent in Japanese and conversational in Hindi and French. Basically, the countries I spend the most time in."

"Ah, makes sense. But you speak Thai often."

"I default to it. It's more comfortable than my supposed native tongue."

"Because of your mother?"

"No, she didn't speak it much, even around me. Before I was apprenticed, I spent many summers with my grandparents in Krung Thep Mahanakhon. After, I visited as often as my master allowed."

Hugh paused for a second, fingers still in the tie's fabric, brows beetled in puzzlement. "I'm sorry, where?"

"What Westerners call Bangkok."

"Oh. Bangkok's not the real name?"

"Not even close. Want to hear the full name of the city?"

"The way you ask that with such a grin makes me think this will be entertaining. All right, tell me."

In a sing-song voice (mostly because that was how they taught the full name to children), Adrien rattled it off. "Kung Thep Mahanakhon Amon Rattanakosin Mahinthara Ayuthaya Mahadilok Phop Noppharat Ratchathani Burirom Udomratchaniwet Mahasathan Amon Piman Awatan Sathit Sakkathattiya Witsanukam Prasit."

Hugh just stared at him for a long second, his expression poleaxed. "You're jesting."

"Totally true. Look it up if you need to verify it with your own eyes. It's the longest city name in the world, or so I'm told. My grandmother told me the story of how it got the name, but to be honest, I don't remember half of it."

Hugh resumed his necktie-tying. "I will find a history book on Thailand when I get back home and learn just why it has such a ridiculously long name. Curiosity compels me."

"Do feel free to remind me afterward. I truly do not remember." Was it just him, or was this the longest anyone had ever taken on a tie?

"I will."

"Hmm, I hope that by year's end, I can return home." Adrien's mouth felt parched around the words.

"Remind me to find another case for you to work on after we're done in Brazil." Hugh finished with the tie—finally!—sliding it up slowly into place, blue eyes locked on Adrien's. "I'm not at all prepared to let go of you."

Damn this man. He really was going to drive Adrien's heart right out of his chest. Did he not understand that he sounded flirtatious? All right, that was likely wishful thinking on Adrien's part, but still. Between the loaded words and the confined space, he was dangerously close to getting the wrong idea.

Pulling free, he cleared his throat and reached for his suit jacket. "You'll likely not get rid of me just yet, anyway. I need to get the boys' reading level up to proficient before I throw another language at their heads."

He fully intended on putting the jacket on himself, but Hugh took it out of his hands, holding the jacket still to help Adrien into it. Adrien's nerves fluttered as he accepted the help, all the while cursing up a storm in his head. He'd have made a stevedore blush.

Surely Hugh had heard the rumors about him. Surely. Men didn't normally come within arm's distance of Adrien when they knew of his nature, so why was—

The thought scattered and flew apart like dust in the wind as those strong hands straightened out his collar, fingers brushing along the nape of his neck, then smoothed down his shoulders, and dammit, that shouldn't feel like a caress. It shouldn't.

It did. Hugh's hands were so warm, even through three layers of cloth. Adrien swallowed hard as lust flitted through his system. *Don't react. Don't react, don't react, don't react, he doesn't mean it that way, he's just…just an affectionate man. That's it, he's merely affectionate.*

The problem was, Adrien was not used to this behavior from a European. The Thai were far more open with each other, more hands-on, more playful. If one of his Thai friends had done that, Adrien wouldn't have thought anything of the behavior.

But dammit, it was a Scotsman doing it, and Hugh shouldn't be this comfortable in Adrien's space.

Adrien stepped away as smoothly as he could muster. It didn't feel at all natural, but hopefully it appeared that way. "Come, Hugh, let's dine. I'm sure the boys are already waiting on us."

"Quite possibly," Hugh said amenably.

Adrien kept his back to the man for as long as possible, fighting the heat in his cheeks because he was *not* blushing. Of course he wasn't. He wasn't some fainting virgin; a simple caress on the shoulders wasn't enough to send him tittering.

Hopefully the walk to the dining room was long enough for him to gain control of himself. His apprentices were far too astute, and he couldn't handle any knowing glances from them right now. He was so jittery that even trying to swallow food was unfathomable to him.

―――❦―――

Hugh walked behind Adrien, giving the man a moment to regain his balance. He hadn't meant to tease him, not at all. Hugh had partially been testing his reactions, trying to ascertain where the line was with Adrien. What he was comfortable with, what would overwhelm him.

In truth, Hugh had mostly just wanted to touch him, no matter how innocent the gesture might be. Adrien was so on guard most of the time, it was hard to approach him, which didn't help Hugh's courting any. He'd capitalized on the opportunity of the moment and waited to see how Adrien would respond.

And oh, what a lovely response it had been.

Adrien had been trying very hard to not show anything, he could tell, but those dark brown eyes had revealed quite a bit. There had been fire, yearning—all quickly banked and repressed. Nothing could quite hide the high color in his pale cheeks, though. It had sparked a low burn in Hugh in response, and he'd wished for nothing more than to press forward. Instinct told him not to, or at least, not yet.

Hugh had suspected since the beginning that the aloof, cool exterior Adrien presented to the world was entirely for show. This was a man who felt much, deeply. His entire being housed powerful emotions, which he chose to reveal only to a select few. Considering how his family had betrayed him, who could blame him?

If Hugh played his cards right, he might earn the privilege to become part of that inner circle. He prayed it turned out that way. The trick would be to convince Adrien he really was flirting with him. That might be more of an uphill battle than he'd initially planned on.

Fortunately, for both their sake, Hugh Quartermain did not know how to quit until he got the results he wanted.

Eight

Sitting on the deck, the shade of the roof overhead keeping the sun out of his eyes, Adrien enjoyed the ocean breeze. It was a touch brisk out here—he might need to go in sooner rather than later—but he was enjoying it too much to move just yet. He'd spent the morning until lunch teaching the boys, and they were on reading exercises now, so he had a bit of time to relax.

A rare thing in Adrien's life. Rare indeed.

The wooden chair next to him creaked a little as another person joined him. Adrien opened one eye enough to see who it was. Hugh gave him a smile as the man settled.

"It's a beautiful day," Hugh said. "Seemed a shame to stay inside."

"It's gorgeous." Adrien let his eyes close. "I quite agree."

"The boys are studying again, I take it?"

"Reading exercises."

"Ahhh."

Adrien had heard about the camera over the past four days—MacMallin had been very enthusiastic in his retelling of it—but he'd yet to hear Hugh's side. "How did the camera turn out, then?"

"Rather well." Hugh propped one ankle over the other, settling in with his hands over his stomach. "Mac's definitely got the knack. I barely had to correct what he was doing, and he did rather well. What I liked best was his enthusiasm for the project. He enjoyed every second of it. It's when a person pursues their passions that they do their best work."

Adrien felt like that should be a slogan, or a motto, as there was truth to it.

"You are a man who enjoys your work," Hugh said, his tone warm, almost...affectionate? Surely Adrien was hearing that wrong. "I can tell not only by how you approach cases handed to you, but by how you teach Julian. You don't have him just memorize spells."

"No, not really much point to it." Adrien liked how Hugh observed things. Damn, but this man really did pay attention. "I mean, you can do the basic work if you know the spells, I won't claim otherwise. But it's rather the difference between a person who painted a portrait while copying a master's or being a master painter yourself. Can you do a replica? Yes, well enough. Does it have the same impact or artistry as the original? Not even close. I don't want Julian to be a copycat. He has the power, the raw talent, to be a grand sorcerer. I will not shortchange him by throwing him formulaic spells to memorize."

"You really think he will surpass you in time?"

"I have no doubt of it. It might not be till his late twenties, since he had such a late start in his apprenticeship, but he definitely will."

"I'm quite keen to watch this play out and see it myself."

So was Adrien. He harbored no jealousy toward his apprentice. Julian had suffered enough in his life—he deserved something to compensate, some talent or blessing to offset his terrible beginnings. Giving Julian the opportunities he rightfully deserved was Adrien's privilege and pleasure.

"I feel you're also much more relaxed now. Found your footing in being a master?"

Adrien almost denied this but then paused. "I think I have? To some degree. I'm not nervous I'm going to royally screw the pooch anymore, at least. You're part of the reason for that."

Hugh pointed a finger toward himself, startled. "Me?"

"Yes, you. I've watched how you interact with MacMallin and realized I'm doing much the same with Julian. It's impossible for you to steer a young man wrong, so if I copy you, I'll be fine."

Hugh snorted a laugh. "You give me far too much credit."

Adrien felt in rare form as he teased, "Nonsense. I'll have you know, I give you just the right amount."

This was not at all believed, as Hugh chuckled.

A comfortable silence fell for a moment, broken by Hugh's question.

"How old were you when you started your apprenticeship? I know some parents hold on to their children until they're ten before finding a master. Or did you start right away?"

Adrien opened his eyes, engaging more in the conversation.

"I'd just turned eight. My magic wasn't out of control, but my parents were both the type to eagerly shuffle their children off to someone else to raise. Giving me to a master early on was to their benefit. I got along quite well with my master, so I didn't complain. Besides, it was then that I met both Anastasia and Cynric, who were a year older."

"Three apprentices at once?"

"Yes. Rather odd, I admit. But my master is an odd sort, truth be told. He actually took in four of us at once, although Oliver was a good five years older than me and more established in his studies. To me, the lessons on magic hardly felt like work. I enjoyed the learning of it immensely."

"I know you're still very close to Anastasia and Cynric, are you with Oliver?"

Adrien's mouth twisted up, regret still a touch bitter. "Ha, no. We started out on very good terms, I considered him a close friend, but my relationship with him soured. I lost him and my master in one fell swoop."

"When the truth of your nature came out." The way Hugh said this, it was not a guess.

Adrien snapped his head around, jaw dropping, almost spluttering. Wait, so Hugh did know about him?

"Why are you so surprised?"

He had to put his jaw back in its socket to answer. "Do you mean to tell me you've known about me this whole time?"

Hugh canted his head just a touch, lips curved up in a hint of a smile. "Well, not from the very beginning, but I did learn something about you mid-sea serpent case, yes." He answered as if it wasn't anything earth shattering.

"And you still don't..." *shy away*?

"Don't...what? Treat you like a leper? Feel wary coming into your personal space? My god, Adrien, is that really how people treat you? Is it so common that you find it the norm?"

Honesty forced him to admit the truth. "Well, yes."

Hugh lifted a hand over his eyes and muttered, "I now understand why you react so."

This revelation turned Adrien's entire conception of Hugh's interactions with him on its head. He'd known. He'd known Adrien liked men, and not only did it not bother him, he felt quite comfortable and at ease with Adrien. How incredibly rare this man was.

Adrien had liked Hugh from the first moment. He'd always had a good impression of the man who'd earned the title of knight. Now, his respect and admiration for his friend went through the roof. A male friend Adrien didn't have to keep his guard up around was a very, very rare thing. He could count such friends on one hand, to be precise. Having another person join those ranks was more precious than finding a sea chest of gold hiding in the back of a closet.

It felt rather like he'd been carrying this giant millstone about his neck only to be told it was no longer necessary to cart it about. The relief of having this secret out in the open, both acknowledged and accepted, was a huge boon. Adrien felt a touch giddy under the release of the burden.

Hugh leaned in, hand on Adrien's arm, speaking in a low tone that had no chance of carrying to the rest of the deck over the sound of the waves crashing against the prow of the ship. His blue eyes were almost penetrating as they met Adrien's. "You do not need to be on guard with me. You do not need to second-guess what's appropriate, or if I might take certain actions or words the wrong way. Just be yourself. Be comfortable with me. Hell, Adrien, you're not even the only friend I have with such inclinations."

Adrien startled all over again, this second wave of surprise hitting almost as strongly as the first. "You're jesting."

"I'm not, I assure you." Hugh sat back a little as he thought. "You'd be the...fourth? That's not including the friends I have who like both genders."

This man was such a rare breed. Adrien really had chosen the right master for MacMallin. Also, the way the boys could read a man was damn near fortunetelling. Adrien had worried when MacMallin first told him that he'd revealed his past employment to Hugh, as it seemed a foolish gamble to take, but apparently he owed the boy an apology, as he'd been quite right in doing so.

When Hugh spoke like this, a kernel of something like hope sparked in Adrien, and he found it harder and harder to squash the feeling. Adrien was still convinced MacMallin's assertation of Hugh being interested in him was wishful thinking. Adrien didn't for one second believe that. It was Hugh's ease with him that made MacMallin read everything all wrong. But the boy's assurance made it hard to fully tamp down his longing, unfortunately, as

Adrien secretly hoped he was right.

Still, even if a lover was impossible, he could freely be himself around Hugh, and that was something he would take without question. He smiled at Hugh without reservation, feeling rather like a sunburst was spinning about in his chest.

"Men like you are a blessing in this world," Adrien told him. "I wish I had met you years ago. I never thought I'd be grateful for sea serpents and the Chechen Brotherhood."

"Neither did I." Hugh smiled, rueful.

After a moment, Hugh turned slightly, orienting himself to face Adrien more fully, and seemed to hesitate as if carefully choosing his next words. For some reason he looked nervous, which piqued Adrien's curiosity. Hugh had been forthright in their conversations thus far.

"Adrien, in truth, I've misstated things a tad. While I do have many friends and some family who are attracted to their own sex, I—"

"Um, Master?"

Adrien turned to see Julian hovering a few feet away, something clutched to his chest—oh dear. That did not look good. "Judging from the state of that charred book in your hand, a spell got away from you."

"Sorry?" Julian winced. "I did try a repair spell, but..."

"It didn't work. It won't. You have to restore the paper before you can repair the damage, so your repertoire of repair spells won't work here, I'm afraid."

Resigned, Adrien shook his head and got up from the chair. "As long as you didn't do damage to anyone else in the process, it's fine. We'll sort this out quickly. I'll be back, Hugh."

"All right."

Hugh watched Adrien and Julian leave, feeling a bit miffed at the broken moment but also relieved the conversation had taken place. He hadn't known how to mention half of his discoveries to Adrien, as he could never seem to find the right moment for them. At least now he'd gotten some of what Adrien needed to know relayed to him.

He'd hoped to reveal his own nature to Adrien, too, but Julian had interrupted with unfortunate timing. Oh well, he'd just need to broach the subject once more. Surely with Adrien now much more relaxed around him, it wouldn't be hard.

But by god was he gloriously attractive. Adrien smiling in pure joy was enough to blind a man. Hugh's heart had stuttered to a stop, and for a minute, he'd honestly forgotten how to breathe. He'd wanted to touch Adrien so badly, to cup those delicate cheekbones, and had only just kept himself in check.

That smile had given him a taste of what it would be like to have Adrien completely unguarded around him, and it only made Hugh hungrier for more. He wanted such smiles on a regular basis. He wanted the luxury of leaning in, tasting that smile for himself, sharing in Adrien's joy. Dammit all, he wanted to be the cause of such joy, too.

Hugh blew out a breath. Steady on, old fellow, steady on, calm down.

He'd made progress this afternoon. Tremendous progress, really, and he should celebrate the milestone. Not focus on how much more he had to go before he could even confess to the man.

Turning back to the ocean view, Hugh took some time to engrave Adrien's glorious smile into his mind. He still had no idea if Adrien would really want to be lovers or not. Hugh took positive encouragement based on how Adrien had reacted when he'd tied the man's tie a few days ago. Still, that could have been lust. While Hugh liked the idea of Adrien being attracted to him, a casual lover wasn't what Hugh wanted.

Once he made his intentions known, convincing Adrien to be in a proper relationship surely wouldn't be so hard.

Right?

Nine

Adrien spent his time getting dressed for dinner with a smile on his face that he simply could not squash. His talk with Hugh yesterday on the deck had freed him from all sorts of worries, and after that, he'd felt so much more relaxed around the man. It was liberating. There was no need to check every word before it left his mouth, question each action before doing it.

To think, Hugh had never judged him from the beginning. Life would be so much more convenient if people wore signs on their person stating what phobias and such they had. An idle fancy, nothing more, sadly.

Still, he had Hugh steadfastly in his corner, belated though that realization might be. Adrien couldn't begrudge his luck. Really, this year had been extraordinarily good to him. First Julian and MacMallin, now Hugh. When he returned to Thailand, he'd have to visit a temple and make merit in thanks. He was not one to take this good fortune for granted.

Such had been his attitude all the last twenty-four hours.

And then he'd been invited into a game of whist by people he barely knew, where bad luck came knocking.

Well. This was rather awkward.

After-dinner entertainment on the ship varied depending on what a person felt inclined to do. Certain rooms were set up for cigars and drinking, others for cards, yet another for dancing as there was a live band playing, and on the fairer nights, games were laid out on the deck. People milled about through those areas as fancy took them.

Adrien had settled for cards in one of the inner rooms, not in the mood to drink or dance. But now that he was here, he rather wished he'd retired to his cabin instead. He, his partner, and two other passengers he could barely put a name to were playing, and the man who was his partner for the game was quite obviously interested in something other than cards.

If Fernsby tried to scoot in closer to him one more time, Adrien might well curse him with warts.

Yes, he had thought a week ago when Hugh assisted him in dressing that he clearly needed sex, but...not with Fernsby. A full-body shudder tried to rack Adrien from head to toe. The man had a face only a mother would love, but that wasn't even the main problem. For one, Fernsby quite clearly didn't bathe on a regular basis—his body odor was questionable. The ocean air coming in through the open windows did nothing to combat it. For another, he rather resembled a mummy's boy. Everyone had encountered the type at least once in their lives. The little boy who liked being pampered by his mother and had never been interested in growing up.

Adrien would quite willingly swallow a bullet rather than sleep with this man. No thank you. A very firm no thank you.

Unfortunately, Adrien was stuck in the game for a while yet. The very second this round ended, he'd excuse himself and flee. He couldn't do it now without drawing unwanted attention. It was only by some miracle the two women playing opposite them at the table hadn't cottoned on, although they were looking a bit green around the gills.

Fernsby leaned in against his shoulder and muttered under his breath, "Game's dragging on a bit, isn't it?"

Adrien managed a tight smile. Hell's bells. It felt interminable. Normally, finding a man with the same inclinations who was attracted to Adrien was a stroke of luck. Right now, it was rotten luck. *Damn* but Adrien wanted to escape this second.

Fernsby took his smile as some kind of positive sign. He should not have. "Say, why don't we find different...entertainment...after this?"

Adrien would rather be stabbed in the eye repeatedly. Thanks for asking. He focused on his turn and laid his cards down, choosing a bad hand with the hopes of losing faster and getting out of this hairy predicament. "Your turn, Fernsby."

"What? Oh, right." Fernsby focused on his cards long enough to pluck two out and throw them carelessly down.

A warm hand Adrien would know anywhere settled on his shoulder. Hugh. Thank all magic. He glanced up to see his friend's face.

Hugh stared at Fernsby with blue eyes resembling shards of ice. The stare was enough to unnerve Fernsby and he swallowed hard, then cleared his throat before focusing very intently on the cards in his hands.

Adrien leaned into the hold with a silent breath of relief. He didn't even know where Hugh had come from, but the knight had picked up on Adrien's discomfort and come in for the rescue. Bless the man's powers of observation. Also bless him for his intimidation factor. He'd gotten Fernsby to back down with just a look, which Adrien had tried and failed to manage.

"Oh, good show, Mrs. Grey!"

Did someone win? Adrien turned back to the ladies and realized Mrs. Grey had put down a winning hand. Thank fuck, he could politely escape now. He stood immediately. "Well, it's been quite the game. Thank you, ladies."

"It was a pleasure," Mrs. Grey assured him, not so subtly hastening toward the exit. "Do play with us again, Mr. Danvers."

"I shall." Not Fernsby, no, definitely not him.

Hugh's hand found the small of his back as he escorted Adrien out of the room. Adrien did not mind it one bit. For one, it gave Fernsby the mistaken impression Hugh was a jealous lover. For another, he could never complain when Hugh touched him. There was something inherently comforting about it, as if Adrien was under the man's protection and care. A rare feeling in Adrien's world.

They went straight out to the open side deck, where no one else gathered, and it was only then Adrien felt his stress and tension drop as he breathed in the fresh sea air.

"Hugh, whatever favor you need from me, you have it."

He chuckled. "I thought I read that situation right. He was rather bold about it, wasn't he?"

"Bold is one word. Unrepentant. Ridiculous. I could think of a dozen words to describe his flirting. I could *not* get him to stop touching me. Cursing the man seemed like a good idea, that's how desperate I was." Adrien turned to lean his back against the rails. In the dim lighting coming from the moon above, he looked at his friend's face. "Your timing was impeccable. My nerves and nose thank you."

Hugh grinned down at him, eyes dancing with laughter. "I could tell you were about to come out of your skin. I did rather give him the impression I was a jealous lover. You don't mind, do you?"

"Yes, it's *such* a hardship for someone to think I have a famous knight of England as my lover," Adrien drawled in full sarcasm. "I'm not sure if I'll survive."

Hugh chuckled, the sound deep and earthy. "Good, I'm glad."

Hearing his laughter, seeing how at ease Hugh was with the idea, it was hard to stop the insidious flood of thoughts. Adrien sometimes chose partners not because he was strongly attracted to them but because he desired companionship keenly. It had been a mistake every time, hence why he'd sworn off men entirely. If he could have someone like Hugh, it wouldn't ever be a mistake. Regretting a relationship with him was unfathomable.

Adrien yearned, sometimes, for a simple touch from this man's hands. Even the lingering warmth at the small of his back didn't seem to be quite enough. In the first week of the voyage, and especially since their talk on the deck yesterday where Hugh had put him so at ease, it had become all too apparent that Adrien's desire for Hugh was growing. He'd have loved to pretend otherwise, to not acknowledge it, but he could no longer deny it. He wanted Hugh Quartermain.

Desired? No question there, either. A brush of the man's hand was enough to send his nerves tingling with delight. The lust was undeniable. What he wanted, though, was something more. But having a dedicated relationship was doomed before it started. Adrien knew that from painful experience. Friendship was one thing, but a lover meant being constantly in the other's company, and it was that which proved impossible. Adrien was too prickly to live with for long. His last partner had made that very clear. He shouldn't wish for more.

But Adrien did. Ardently.

He told himself, again, that he had far more than he'd ever dared hope for. Hugh being so utterly at ease with him that he would willingly play at being Adrien's lover was a miracle in and of itself. Adrien needed to be wise, to accept what was already freely given and not be greedy.

Damn hard to do it, though. Damn hard.

He put the wistfulness sharply aside and focused on the moment. "Did you come looking for me for a reason?"

"Well, actually, I did have a question for you. If this is a delicate subject, just say so, I'll stop." Hugh cleared his throat a mite before speaking, each word laid out deliberately as if he built a path with them. "Mac told me of his history, I know how you found the boys, and because of that I often give allowances. This might be one of those times I need to, I don't know. I've found the boys on more than one occasion sharing a bed."

Ahhhh. "I don't think they're actively sleeping with each other, if that's what you're asking."

"That's precisely what I'm asking."

"It gave me a turn, too, the first week I had them. I wasn't sure what to make of it. What I have finally figured out is that it's a comfort thing for them." Adrien smiled, expression wry and sad. "When I found them, you see, their sleeping space was up in an attic. They slept together for warmth."

Hugh's eyes closed in understanding.

"I think they also slept together for safety. It's habit, an ingrained one, and frankly speaking, I don't see the harm for now. Especially since they typically have a dog sleeping with them." Adrien eyed him, wondering if there would be an objection. He didn't expect one.

"No, I don't see the harm." Hugh blew out a breath, turning to put his hands on the rails, arm pressed up against Adrien's. "I do worry a bit for the future, when I take Mac with me."

"I agree they'll need to break the habit one day. They'll have lives and future lovers of their own. For now, let them be. They'll gradually outgrow it." Adrien had no interest in hurrying that process along. The busy life of an adult would do that soon enough.

"Truly, they likely will. It does beg the question. Have you had one?" Hugh asked him. "A proper lover."

"Not for years now. My last attempt at a dedicated relationship backfired rather spectacularly. After that, I had dalliances. There was a friend in Thailand whom I sometimes indulged with. It was a mutually beneficial relationship, nothing like a committed one, and that's recently run its course." Adrien snorted, no humor whatsoever in the sound. "I'm too prickly to be good company for long, and I move about with no notice, both of which stumps a potential lover."

"I really do need a list of whoever it was who convinced you you're bad company." An edge of hard steel crept into Hugh's words. He didn't look pleased, his jaw working. "I'd like to have a chat with them."

For some reason, Adrien felt there might be whips and iron maidens involved in that chat. It made him smile to see Hugh so defensive of him. Truly, this man was loyal to a fault. "Not everyone has your good humor and patience, Hugh."

Hugh leaned into him even more, their arms now overlapping, his words a warm burr in the night air. "You are ever worth the trouble. Worth the risk. I will convince you of this come hell or high water."

Dammit, this man was determined to undermine Adrien's resolve to remain single. How was he supposed to respond when Hugh said things like that, with such earnest conviction? What he wanted to do and what he should do were two entirely different things. He wanted to tell Hugh to not say such honeyed words. They gave a man all sorts of wrong impressions. But he wanted to hear those words too, so he bit his tongue.

"It doesn't look like you believe me right now." Hugh gave an enigmatic smile—difficult to read, but it made Adrien swallow hard for some reason. "Just wait. One day, you'll believe me."

"I believe that you mean it, that I'm worth the trouble," Adrien offered. It was even the truth.

"Well," Hugh murmured, "that's progress of sorts, and good enough for tonight, I suppose."

Adrien pulled his eyes away, afraid he really was going to do something stupid if they lingered out here. The darkness gave the illusion of privacy, which wasn't at all the case. People were just beyond the door. This bubble he occupied, indulging in Hugh's company, was a dangerous place. He wished for it to last forever, but of course it couldn't possibly. "How about we go in? I could use a drink."

"As you like."

Just one drink, though. Adrien absolutely did not trust himself around Hugh Quartermain while intoxicated and craving his touch. That was a recipe for disaster if he'd ever heard one.

Ten

Hugh looked about the Brazilian city of Macapá with an air of relief. Finally, after three weeks of travel, they had reached the hotel. They'd made it to port late afternoon in Rio de Janeiro, gathered up trunks and suitcases, then Adrien had found a conveniently unused door and portaled them straight north to Macapá. Hugh had been a bit worried about portaling the distance—it meant crossing half of Brazil—but Adrien had just given him a cheeky wink and assured him that the mithril on his wrist would adequately compensate.

It did seem to, in fact. Adrien didn't even look winded upon arrival. Hugh was secretly thrilled, too, that Adrien so clearly liked the cuff he'd made. He'd worn it constantly since receiving it weeks ago and was not the least shy about doing so. Hugh really, truly wanted to take that as a positive sign. Surely it meant Adrien returned his affections to some degree? Hugh had never found another private moment to tell Adrien that his nature aligned with Adrien's. He'd never been able to tell the man he liked him and wanted to be lovers, and the lack of opportunity grated sorely. Short of ambushing Adrien and taking off with him for a few hours, he couldn't figure out how to manage it.

Unfortunately, Hugh was out of time to contemplate, as he now had to focus on the task at hand.

Hugh had made arrangements with the Amazon Pier for a night's stay; he'd been to the hotel before and knew it to have good service. Adrien had portaled them straight to the lobby, using the front door to step through.

Magic was damned convenient sometimes.

The front desk clerk startled to see four foreign men suddenly appear with luggage in tow, but she rallied quickly, giving them a smile. "Welcome, gentlemen."

Hugh kept his suitcase in hand as he crossed over the tiles

and gave her an answering smile. "I've a reservation under Hugh Quartermain."

She flipped her book's pages, running a manicured finger down the page before giving a nod. In charmingly accented English she asked, "Yes, for three rooms? Overnight stay?"

"Correct."

"Please leave your luggage here, and I will have someone bring it up." She turned to the board behind her filled with keys and fetched three down before passing them over. "Your rooms are on the second story, bay view."

"Thank you." Hugh took the keys and retreated to where the other three waited, handing them over. He spoke as he handed each key over. "I've a business associate I want to contact before we go for dinner. Boys, I booked a room for you to share, so this is your key. Adrien, I'd prefer it if you'd sit in on this conversation. I'm sure you have questions to ask Ribeiro."

"That I do." Adrien took the key and pocketed it.

"Very good. I'll give him a ring."

There was a phone table right there in the foyer, meant for guests, and Hugh picked up the receiver before dialing in the operator.

"*Operador falando,*" a whisky-rich female voice said.

Hugh's Portuguese was limited but he could manage this much. "Afonso Ribeiro, *por favor.*"

"*Por favor, espere.*"

He waited, but not long, the call connecting quickly.

"*Olá,*" Ribeiro answered in his gruff voice, sounding distracted.

"Ribeiro, it's Hugh Quartermain. I'm here in Macapá."

Ribeiro switched to English, sounding…stressed, which was never a good sign. "*Quartermain, you made good time, and it's just as well. Nothing good happened since my last telegram to you.*"

Hugh internally groaned. "I didn't expect things to improve, but have they gotten worse?"

"*Unfortunately.*"

"Can you come to the hotel? I brought a sorcerer with me, a damn fine one, and I hope to sort things out with his help. Come have dinner with us and fill me in on the latest."

"*Which hotel, same as last time?*"

"Same one."

"I'll be there shortly."

"Good." Hugh hung up and then let his head hang for a moment. Damn and blast, how could things have possibly gotten worse?

Adrien stepped in closer and gave him a concerned look. "Bad news already?"

"Unfortunately. Ribeiro said nothing good has happened since his last telegram to me. I cannot imagine what else has gone wrong since nothing was going right to begin with."

"I'll help you resolve this," Adrien said with a small smile. "Buck up."

"I know you will. But I'd hoped to not drag you into such a mess, too." With a shake of his head, Hugh rose from the small phone table and gestured to the dining room within view of the lobby. "Shall we go and reserve a table? Ribeiro should be here shortly."

"I'm quite famished so that sounds lovely. The boys are guiding the porter to put the right bags in the right rooms, then they'll join us."

The dining room was nicely appointed, with stark white tablecloths over the round tables and ceiling fans lazily spinning overhead to combat the heat. A waitress came by to take their drink orders, and Hugh unapologetically ordered a white wine. He refused to have this conversation without something to ease the pain. Everyone more or less met at the dining table at the same time, the boys coming in first, with Ribeiro right on their heels.

Ribeiro was a native of Brazil through and through, with olive skin and thick black hair. He had an affable look to him—the wide face, curved belly, and full beard giving him a soft impression. It was an utter lie, of course; the man was ruthless when it came to business. Behind that kind smile was a very shrewd mind. Hugh had Ribeiro as a business partner here in Brazil for a reason.

Ribeiro regarded everyone with a blink, the two teenagers especially, obviously not quite sure what to make of them. Hugh stepped in to do introductions. "Ribeiro, this is Adrien Danvers, the sorcerer I mentioned."

He offered a hand, taking Adrien in from head to toe in curiosity. "Sorcerer. You're very welcome here. We need good help."

"Thank you. Kindly said. I hope I can resolve this." Adrien

shook the man's hand firmly before letting go.

"This is Julian, Adrien's apprentice," Hugh said, "and MacMallin, my apprentice."

Ribeiro shook their hands, but his hold on MacMallin lingered. "Your master kept saying 'no apprentice, no apprentice, too busy for an apprentice,' so *you* must be very smart to catch his eye. I look forward to knowing you better."

MacMallin ducked his head, and was that a blush on the boy's cheeks? "Thank you, sir. I'm very new to it all, so be gentle with me, please."

"You do fine, I think. Polite men always do well." Ribeiro gave a nod and let go. "All right, sit, sit. Let me tell you what circus we now have."

Hugh sat, as did everyone else, Ribeiro staying on his right to converse better. "I have wine coming."

"For this, we need whole crate of wine." Ribeiro looked fit to be tied as he unbuttoned his linen suit coat in order to sit comfortably. "All right. Last I spoke with you, I shut down worksite temporarily, afraid for crews, yes?"

"Right." Hugh didn't like this bleak start.

"So, since then, we have two things rear heads." Ribeiro talked with his hands as he spoke, getting more agitated with each word. "First, Americans."

Adrien stirred. "I'm sorry, this is an issue?"

"Americans don't agree with our claim to worksite. They try and take over." Ribeiro snorted. "I send letters to embassy, nothing. I talk with foreman directly, nothing. They insist they have the right to work it since we won't. I tell them we are working on it, just waiting on crews to come in, they still try to go in. I honestly think they already sent men in. More and more Americans are coming in, and they're bringing Chinese workers, too, and you don't do that unless actively working site."

Hugh's wine needed to get here sooner rather than later. He could feel the headache brewing already in his temples. "You're telling me I'm going to have to battle someone else already working my site before we can even get in to investigate?"

"*Sí*. It stupid, but that's what I'm saying."

"I thought no one could work the site without being killed?" Adrien objected. "So how are they managing?"

"I don't know if they are." Ribeiro spread his hands in a shrug.

"They keep bringing more and more workers, I never see anyone come back, so I think people are getting killed. But they're not stopping."

"Which company is doing this, do you know?" Hugh had American connections. He might be able to work this out somehow.

"No one tell me. They just dismiss me, very rude."

"All right, let me tackle that, then. I'll try and find out, see if I can stop them." Hugh paused as the wine and water glasses arrived, accepting a glass gratefully. He let it breathe for a moment as he asked, "What else? Is it just the Americans causing trouble?"

"Ha, no, that would be walk in park. Too easy." Ribeiro rolled his eyes, looking very put upon and murderous. "No, we finally figure out two days ago what was killing people. Mapinguari claim that land."

"I'm sorry, what?" Hugh had never heard of the like.

Adrien, beside him, groaned and put his head into his hand.

"Your sorcerer knows what these are." Ribeiro jerked his chin toward Adrien.

"I really wish I didn't." Adrien took a sip of his wine, as if needing the alcohol to brace himself. "I've encountered them once before and damn near didn't survive the fight. Julian, take note of this, I do not want you to *ever* go into the Amazon Rainforest on your own. Bring an experienced team with you if you must. There's many a reason for it, and the Mapinguari are one of them."

Julian gave a game nod. "But what are they?"

"A headache. Shortly mine. A Mapinguari stands about seven feet tall, covered in long, matted fur. It looks rather like a giant bear with a monkey's face, but it has a second mouth in its belly. The stench is horrific, enough to make anyone within range nauseated. People often become so ill due to the smell that they can't effectively fight. It can scream in such a horrific way that most men's nerves break and they run in the other direction. Much good that does them, as the Mapinguari are incredibly fast. The only way to kill it is to shoot it in the head—which is almost impossible to do as it's both quick and, if you come in too close, you become dizzy and disoriented. It's known to be very, very territorial. It's no wonder, Hugh, that you've lost multiple work crews. Mapinguari kill anything in their territory without mercy."

Ribeiro lifted his glass in a toast to Adrien. "You, sir, know your business. Quartermain, you bring right expert with you.

Now, question is, will you hunt?"

"Not alone, I won't." Adrien's answer was blunt and firm. "I refuse to take my apprentice in there, though; he's not seasoned enough for such a hunt."

Julian objected. "I helped with the sea monster!"

"Based on what they're describing, it's a different story here, lad," Hugh said gently. "For one, you can't attack it from a distance. The rainforest is incredibly dense, you won't have the sight lines. For another, you'll be fighting it right on its own turf. I don't think either of you should go in with us."

Both MacMallin and Julian looked disappointed, their shoulders slumping.

"I insist they do not." Adrien turned to Hugh, jaw set with determination. "I want to call in Anastasia and Cyn. She can help with the boys. I know she won't mind, as she's already agreed in the event she was needed. Cynric, on the other hand, is the hunter I need for this."

"Done." Hugh wasn't about to argue with his expert, and he also had no interest in putting Adrien at risk. If Adrien refused to tackle this without backup, then backup he would have.

Since neither Julian nor MacMallin looked pleased about this, Hugh offered an olive branch. "You can help me in other ways, with Adrien's approval. We need to know which company sent the Americans down here and how many workers they've sent in."

Adrien pondered for a moment before nodding. But for some reason, he pointed a stern finger at them. "Talking only."

MacMallin blinked ingenuous eyes at him. "There *are* other ways of gathering information—"

"Do not make me repeat myself."

What other way...oh. Right. Former occupation as a prostitute. Damn, Hugh would have to keep an eye on him.

Adrien, with a weather eye on MacMallin—as if he didn't trust him—pulled out a compact mirror from his breast pocket. He uttered a quick call spell before speaking distinctly. "Cynric."

There was a grumbling sound, rather like a person who had been yanked out of some activity and wasn't pleased about it. *"Why do you always call me when I'm either eating or sleeping?"*

"Incredible timing," Adrien deadpanned. "Pay attention. I need you."

"It best not be another sea serpent."

"No, worse."

"*What can possibly be worse than giant fishies wanting to eat me?*"

Adrien cocked a brow in challenge. "Mapinguari."

There was a moment of dead silence.

"*Shit. You're in Brazil already, aren't you?*"

"I am, yes. Macapá."

"*I need three days. Maybe two. I'm in the middle of something, then I'm coming. Is Hugh nearby?*"

Hugh leaned over to speak into the mirror. "Hello, Cynric."

"*Damn, I can't talk Adrien out of this if the job's for you. All right, all right, I'm definitely coming. Just don't go in there without me.*"

"I'm not that suicidal." Adrien's voice was dry as a martini. "I still vividly remember our last excursion into the rainforest."

"*Yes, thank you for bringing that up. I'd almost successfully suppressed that memory. Wait, tell me you're not taking the boys in there.*"

"I'm not an idiot, Cyn. I'll go in to establish a portal and then come straight back out. I promise you, I will not linger, nor go looking for trouble. I'll call Anastasia next. If she won't come here to watch them, I'll portal them home first."

"*Phew, good. Glad you're being sensible. Let me finish killing something, board my dog, and I'll be right with you. Stay safe.*"

Hugh did feel better about Cynric coming. He'd seen the man's skills, after all; he knew how capable of a fighter he was. This situation was treacherous as it stood. It could only improve with Cynric's presence.

Adrien handed the mirror over to Julian. "On second thought, you call Anastasia and give her the rundown. Me, she'll argue with. You, she'll do anything for."

That was the better tactic. It wasn't manipulation so much as playing to favorites, and Anastasia clearly favored Julian. How Adrien managed to keep Julian as his apprentice was anyone's guess, as Anastasia would have dearly loved to have him.

Ribeiro leaned in to murmur near Hugh's ear, "These people, they are skilled?"

"Some of the best." Fortunately. Hugh would shortly need every ounce of skill and knowledge they could bring to the table.

This manganese was really proving to be a lot of trouble.

Eleven

Anastasia showed up in the lobby of the hotel within the hour, with four ingots of mithril to aid in her portaling such an insane distance. She had a single suitcase in hand, a bag over her shoulder, and an irate look upon her face. Well, irate and tired. It was midnight her time, after all, and here she'd traveled across the ocean in one leap to boot. She was bound to be fatigued. She also had Cynric's dog, for some reason.

She looked at Adrien as if he were somehow to blame for all of this. Which, fair.

He put on a smile and dangled a room key in the air. "I have an ocean-side room for you."

"At least you know how to compensate me."

"Why do you have Captain?"

"Cynric said he was going to board him." Anastasia sniffed. "The absolute *gall*. Poor Captain would view it as a punishment. He hates being away from his people."

Well, she was right about that. Collies adored their people and didn't like it when separated.

Suspicious, she demanded, "You didn't do that with Darby, did you?"

"Of course not. My cousin George and his wife are watching her. She was having a blast playing with their children when I left."

"At least you have good sense."

Captain pulled free of her to get scratches from Adrien, which he obliged. Since last seeing the pup, he'd clearly grown. Still was all fluff and ears, though.

Anastasia handed off her luggage to a bellboy, then Adrien led her out onto the back patio. With the shade provided there and the ocean breeze, it was quite pleasant. It was also where everyone had chosen to have dessert.

"Captain!" Julian greeted the dog with a wide smile. "Hey,

boy."

The sable collie bounded joyfully to him, as Julian was a favorite of Captain's.

Anastasia greeted everyone—being properly introduced to Ribeiro in the process—then was offered dessert as well, which she happily accepted. She settled at their table. "Take Captain for a quick walk, would you?" she asked the boys.

"Sure," MacMallin said. "He probably wants to sniff everything and get territory down anyway. Come on, Cap!"

Anastasia looked between the three men. "Now. Fill me in. Has anything changed in the past hour?"

"Not really. We're trying to work out the logistics of this." Hugh pressed a finger and thumb to the bridge of his nose, stress clear in his expression. "Ribeiro needs to stay here to keep our business going, and—"

"I'm not a fighter," Ribeiro said firmly. "You leave me out of Mapinguari business."

Hugh held up his hands in a placating manner. "Peace, Ribeiro. I meant I need you in Macapá to field new information. I have no intention of putting you at such risk."

Adrien refused to take him along anyway if he didn't even have the skills to defend himself. That was madness. "I'm also concerned about trying to portal to the worksite."

Anastasia blinked at him. "Is that even a possibility?"

"Hmm. There are buildings there," Hugh said. "We had something of a makeshift camp established before all hell broke loose."

"Ah. But Julian mentioned when he called that the Americans might be there, which is why portaling in is likely a bad idea."

"Now you've got it." Adrien slumped back into his seat with an aggravated sigh. "I don't dare take that risk. I mean, bad enough the Mapinguari are in that area, but Americans? We have no idea what they've done there. It would be like portaling into a beehive and hoping not to be stung. Only possibility I see is to stick with our original travel plan of going in by boat."

Anastasia had her thinking cap on. "Get in as close as you dare, then build a doorway and portal Cynric through. How long would that take?"

"Two, three days," Ribeiro said. "Depending on weather and such. They can take a riverboat straight there."

"In two or three days, Cynric should be able to join you," Anastasia pointed out. "The timing should work out very fine indeed."

It was true, that was the case. Adrien looked to Ribeiro, who knew the area far better than he did. "Is it possible to book passage on a boat for tomorrow?"

Ribeiro grunted. "Easy, easy. Most boats leave early morning. You ready for that?"

"I can be." Adrien moved about with little to no notice most days, so leaving at dawn was no real challenge. "Hugh, what do you think?"

"I think it the sensible approach, and truly, I want this resolved sooner rather than later. But I'm uneasy about going in when I don't know who these Americans are. The Mapinguari, at least, are a predictable danger."

"We can go and ascertain for ourselves." Adrien shrugged. "It's the most direct method, and if the Americans prove hostile, I'll just portal us back and we can return with a larger force."

"Well, when you put it that way..." Hugh gave him a quick smile. "Ribeiro, looks like we need to book that passage after all."

"Come with me, then. If we're to get you on, must talk to a riverboat captain tonight."

Hugh stood. "I'll be back."

The two men left, heading for the city, and they were no sooner out of earshot than Anastasia leaned in with a wicked smile. "Soooo I noticed the two of you are much more at ease with each other. Have you realized yet that you like him?"

Adrien sighed. This was going to be a very long evening.

Their sudden plans had Adrien and Hugh boarding a riverboat the next morning, heading inland toward the rainforest proper. Well, really, it was a steamboat with massive paddles on the back end. It stood three decks tall, the topmost one an open deck with a roof, with living quarters—such as they were—on the second deck. The bottom was given over to the engine, kitchen, and what storage was available. If not for the deck jutting out front, it would resemble nothing more than a rectangular box floating down the river. A brightly painted blue one, no less.

As soon as they had their luggage on board, they retreated to the top deck, which was the only place that promised something like coolness and shade.

Anyone who had spent time in the jungle could tell you the Amazon was beastly hot. Humid, too—enough to make the back of a person's neck constantly damp. Adrien didn't even try to wear a proper English suit out in this environment. He'd burn up within minutes. Instead, he'd switched to local dress, which consisted of a long-sleeved dress shirt, wide brimmed hat to keep off the sun, and loose-fitting pants that tucked into shin-high boots. Marginally cooler and it kept the mosquitos off when he didn't have a charm handy.

Hugh had adopted the same mode of dress and looked honestly quite dashing in it. Then again, any clothes seemed to suit him. Adrien was willing to bet no clothes would suit him even better.

Adrien eyed that thought sideways, fully suspect. After the three-week voyage here, he had finally admitted to himself that he was strongly attracted to Hugh Quartermain. Adrien didn't want him as just a friend. Apparently, his subconscious had taken that capitulation and run with it because he now found himself harboring a crush. Which was entirely unhelpful. Adrien had the devil of a time keeping himself in check as it was.

Why must Hugh be such a charming gentleman? The man was irresistible.

Hugh sipped his water. "The boys were clearly disappointed about not going with us, but in truth, I'm glad they stayed behind. I'd worry about them the entire time."

"I know precisely what we're up against with the Mapinguari. There is no way in hell I will put them at that kind of risk. Not to mention the additional intruders we're now facing."

"Agreed." Hugh turned his face forward for a moment, eyes closed. "The spray from the water is helping to cool things down some. I don't look forward to the moment we're off the water. It gets beastly hot quickly."

"Well, if you weren't traveling with me, it would." Adrien smirked a bit as he threw a spell at the base of Hugh's water glass.

Suspiciously, Hugh lifted the glass again and sipped from it. Delight spread over his face, lips turning up at the corners. "You chilled the glass. Adrien, may I take you into jungles with me from now on?"

"If you insist." Adrien hid his glee behind his own glass as he took a sip.

"I'm quite curious, actually, since you've mentioned being in this rainforest before." Hugh set his glass down on the table, leaning forward in his wooden folding chair to face Adrien more directly. "How and when did you face a Mapinguari?"

"This story is not to be told to either Julian or MacMallin," Adrien said in warning. "It'll only make them more upset."

"You were their age, I take it."

"Nearabouts. I was two years older than them, a precocious sixteen."

Hugh chuckled, blue eyes twinkling. "No, we absolutely shouldn't tell them that. There would be outrage. It's not the same thing, of course. You had nearly a decade of magical training under your belt by that point."

"More or less. Julian has barely had half a year of training. Still, they'll hear the age and be quite cross." Shaking his head, Adrien moved on to the story itself. "It was one of the last group expeditions we did together, in fact. My master was called in for help and since we were all more or less trained at that point, he took us in with him. Us being myself, Cynric, and Anastasia."

"Not the other apprentice you mentioned before?"

"No, Oliver was licensed and out on his own at that point. Anyway, us four traveled to South America to work the case. A ranch developer who wanted to grow soybeans had been trying and failing to establish a ranch for nearly a year before he called us in. All because the Mapinguari kept killing anyone working the area. The natives didn't want to help because, of course, they want to keep the Amazon as it is."

Hugh acknowledged this with a tip of his head. "I'm rather in the same boat, so I understand the situation. And then?"

"It was madness from day one, really. The very moment we stepped foot in the rainforest, we were besieged. There's all manners of creatures up here, but the ones that caused us the most trouble were the Iara and the thrice-cursed Mapinguari." Just the memory of it gave Adrien a headache, and he rubbed his forehead with his fingertips. "The first night, we camped at the river's edge. The Iara, or mermaids as most know them, tried to seduce Cynric into coming to the water. The rest of our time here went downhill from there."

Hugh sipped at his water. "Has he ever lived that down?"

"Anastasia had to rescue him. No"—Adrien laughed— "she has never let him live it down. That said, Hugh, do keep close to me while we're on land. I don't want you running afoul of the mermaids."

"This is actually the first I've heard of them," Hugh said. "Which I find interesting, as I've been through this area before."

"You were lucky to not run into them."

"Apparently. Either that or my guides were that good at protecting me without my realizing. How are they dangerous? Do they like to drown people?"

"And eat them."

"Oh. Charming."

"Indeed."

Judging from Hugh's face, he looked as pleased with this information as he would finding a roach in his food. It begged the question.

"You're quite sure the manganese is worth it?"

Hugh grimaced, shoulders slumping for a moment. "Largest unclaimed deposit I've found in the world. Trust me, if there was another source, I wouldn't be wrestling with this one."

"Fair enough."

They weren't the only people on the boat, of course, because the four-man crew was also with them. The boat was mostly doing a supply run, going down the river and dropping cargo off on the way. A slower approach than traveling straight there, but it had been the only boat going in the right direction this week, so it was the one Hugh had bought passage on.

That said, no one sane stayed on the river in the dead of night. It wasn't safe to do so. The captain pulled into a dock near one of the many indigenous villages along the riverbank. They were off-loading crates of cargo, with the intent of staying there for the evening. Adrien left his luggage on the boat, taking only the necessities with him as they disembarked.

Dealing with Mapinguari and Dogged Engineers 83

Villages in the rainforest were timeless in a sense. They never really changed in appearance. They had, at most, a population of about five hundred—or so was Adrien's experience. This one looked a bit smaller than that. The huts were all on stilts, a good three feet off the ground, and made of clapboard and thatch roofs. Only one of them was different; it had a conical shape and an open-air second story. It must be the gathering hall, or something along those lines.

Mixed in with the humid air was the scent of spices and cook fires, which made sense, as it was late in the evening and time for dinner. Adrien followed their captain, Cruz, along the narrow wooden walkway, the boards clacking a bit in places.

Cruz stopped at the first hut and pointed toward it. "Dinner will be brought to you. That's our stay for the night."

Adrien regarded the single-room dwelling, the door open but with a mosquito net hanging inside the doorway to keep the insects out, and pursed his lips. Hmm. No hint of a bed or mattress, but at least there was a wooden floor. And it was on stilts, so if the river rose during the night, they'd be all right. He'd slept in worse.

"Thank you, Captain. Anything in particular to watch out for in this area? I know the Bouina, Boto, and Iara are generally along the river. Anything else?"

Cruz was a veteran captain, naturally dusky skin even darker because of so much time on the water, and he pushed his hat back to give Adrien a long, thoughtful look. "You know about those?"

"Not the first time I've been in the Amazon."

"Huh. That's the ones to watch out for. Them and mosquitos."

Oh, the mosquitos wouldn't get much of a chance. Adrien had an excellent repellant. "Then I'll keep watch for those. Thank you."

Cruz gave him another considering look before nodding and moving on.

Ascending the stairs, Adrien put his bag inside. He gave Anastasia a quick call using his monocle to check in and update her on their progress, but the conversation didn't last five minutes. He had expected Hugh to join him well before the call was over, but he didn't. Now where had Hugh gotten himself off to? He'd been right behind Adrien, or so he'd thought. He could well have forgotten something on the boat and doubled back to get it, but Adrien didn't like having him out of sight in a target-rich environment.

Uneasy, he walked back along the sidewalk toward the boat. Surely Hugh was somewhere along here.

There was a line of trees breaking up the area before the clear spot near the riverbank itself. The second Adrien got past that line of trees, he spotted familiar copper hair. Hugh was speaking with a woman near the riverbank, shaking his head at something she said. Her hand was on his arm, body language imploring him to follow, a charming smile on her face.

To any layman, she was a native woman who liked the look of this foreign man.

Adrien took one look at her and hissed in outrage. Iara! Hell's bells, a damn river mermaid was trying to seduce Hugh.

Anger flashed hot through his veins and he stomped forward. Adrien summoned a fallen tree branch lying nearby with nothing more than a flick of his fingers, bringing it right into his palm. He forged the spell around it, then shot it forward, as fast as any bullet.

The branch hit its target with a sickening thud, sinking right into her chest and killing her in one blow. She gurgled for a moment, eyes wide in shock, before slumping over sideways, hitting the sandy area with a hard thud.

Hugh jumped as she fell back, hand already on his Webley revolver, spinning about to see the attacker—only to stop, brows beetled in confusion. "Adrien?"

"That," Adrien said, still stomping forward because his anger had not dissipated completely, "was an Iara. A river mermaid."

"Oh. But she…" Hugh looked down at the body. In death, her glamour had fallen away, the human disguise shed as she reverted to her mermaid appearance. The large fin and gills along her ribs rather gave it all away. Hugh's jaw dangled for a moment before closing with a snap. "I did not realize they could change forms like that."

"They can, yes. They can't get far from the river, so it's not as much of a concern once you're in the village proper, but they can be quite deceptive."

Adrien took hold of Hugh under the guise of looking him over. In truth, he was still rattled, and he needed to somehow ground himself. Damn, that had been close. Another minute or two, and Hugh might well have been at the bottom of the river.

"I couldn't understand what she was saying, and she wouldn't let go of me, so I thought to humor her until one of the crew passed me and could interpret." Hugh ran a hand over his jaw, expression disturbed. He took Adrien's hand, squeezing it once, the palm warm and calloused. "More fool me. Thank you, Adrien."

"Please don't be such a gentleman. Too many things out here can disguise themselves as human and cause you trouble—if not outright kill and eat you."

Adrien almost didn't do it, because it wasn't in his nature to keep hold of, well, anyone, but Hugh had told him several times to not curb his instincts. That he was comfortable with Adrien. He chose to take the man at his word and looped arms with him before drawing him back toward the village.

"Come. We've dinner that will be served to us shortly. You have everything off the boat you want for the night?"

Hugh put his hand over Adrien's, keeping it in place. "I do not. I was distracted by her before I could collect it. Escort me?"

"Of course."

Adrien reveled in walking arm in arm with Hugh. He'd never experienced this with a man. To have that warm, calloused hand over his also thrilled him on some level. The inherent strength in Hugh was obvious when in contact with him, and part of Adrien's mind took this information and formed all sorts of fantasies with it. Those warm hands would feel delightful sweeping along his skin, and having the man's weight on him would be perfectly delicious.

Adrien mentally reined in his libido before it could get lost in such fancies. Look at him, getting butterflies in his stomach just because a man touched his hand. He was worse than a schoolboy with a crush.

But, well, he couldn't help the feeling. For once, Adrien chose not to chastise himself, but to enjoy it instead. He'd vanquished a mermaid and defended the knight, after all, so a reward was due, wasn't it?

Smiling to himself, he kept stride with Hugh as they retreated to the boat.

TWELVE

Hugh gradually came awake, senses filtering in different impressions as he rose into consciousness. The sound of birdsong from outside, the blanket over him, the touch of coolness brushing over his exposed skin—and the warm weight of another person cuddled against his chest.

Wait, that last part didn't make sense.

He put more effort into opening his eyes and looked down. Oh. Oh my. How incredibly cute was this? At some point in the night, Adrien had rolled closer and snuggled in, with his head pillowed on Hugh's outstretched arm. Hugh had absolutely no feeling in that arm but wasn't about to complain. Adrien trusting him enough to curl up against his side, even if it had been done in sleep, thrilled him.

It also might well have been the cold sending him closer. Adrien had improved their accommodations last night using a variety of spells. He'd put a mosquito repellant charm on the roof, applied cushioning spells to their bedrolls, then another charm against the wall to chill the air and make it comfortable enough to sleep. The small one-room hut hadn't been meant for just the two of them, but also the four-man crew, which made for very crowded conditions. Still, the place could hold six men at a stretch.

Especially when Adrien tucked himself against Hugh like this.

Even in the dim lighting of the cabin, the younger man's beauty was apparent. Normally, Adrien kept his black hair slicked away from his face, but right now it lay loose against his forehead and cheek, a high contrast against his fair skin. Without any need to hide, Hugh could look over his features at his leisure, drinking him in. He could see how guarded Adrien was on a daily basis, because in sleep he looked far more innocent. Younger. It made Hugh ache, wishing he could see this peace on Adrien's face even while awake.

Hugh's preference would be to stay like this the rest of the day, as ridiculous as that might sound. He couldn't help but wish for it. Since their acquaintance, Adrien's guard had slowly come down. The wary, uptight creature Hugh had first met was nowhere in sight now when Adrien was with him. Lately, the sorcerer easily conversed, answered questions, and shared his background without evasion. Moments when Adrien trusted him enough to come in close made Hugh happy. Adrien now lingered in Hugh's personal space without apology and was increasingly flustered around him. Hugh liked the response, the blatant attraction, when he touched the man and saw the slight blush in those fair cheeks.

Would they ever get the chance to become lovers? Waking up to Adrien's solid heat and weight pressed against him sparked a deep lust and need in his libido. Which was hardly helpful in a room full of other people, but Hugh couldn't control his desire for the sorcerer. Just the touch of the man's hand sent delicious sparks of pleasure through him. But being able to hold him like this? Irresistible. And dangerous, as it tempted Hugh to push more boundaries. Hugh had seen glimpses of Adrien's own desire, knew he trusted him, but something held the sorcerer back from taking the leap beyond friendship. It seemed the boys had called it correctly—no matter how Adrien might feel, he would not make the first move. He was too accustomed to rejection and, out of fear, wouldn't put any effort into changing their relationship from what it was now. Hugh would happily destroy that fear and sweep this precious man up into his arms, never to let go.

It made his heart ache to think that this good man had been hurt so many times that he would no longer try for anything. It seemed entirely unfair that the world would be so cruel to someone who was kind by nature. Hugh would rail against it, but that seemed a wasted effort. All he could do now was protect Adrien, give him a safe place to rest his heart. Hugh could be that for him.

Assuming he could ever find a moment alone with Adrien without the possibility of interruption. That was a hard thing to manage. It seemed they were ever surrounded by people or out in the open where people could wander by without notice. Made it damn hard to confess. Hugh didn't see the situation improving, even out here in the rainforest. This morning gave him a glimpse of what could be, and the patience that had led him this far abruptly abandoned him. Hugh was a man of action, first and foremost, and perhaps it was time he made his affection for Adrien more obvious. Without cornering him, of course; Hugh didn't want to do that. How he'd manage that balance, he wasn't sure.

He'd find a way to do it, though. He would. Hugh would not let this state of limbo cage them for much longer. Even if Adrien refused him, Hugh wanted to at least convey to him that he was wanted. If nothing else, Hugh would make sure that happened.

People started to stir, waking up and nudging each other awake. Hugh didn't wish for them to catch Adrien like this, as it would only embarrass him, so he regretfully patted Adrien's shoulder as well.

"Adrien? Danvers, wake up."

Adrien sucked in a breath as he awoke, eyes fluttering open. The moment he became fully awake was apparent as he froze, body stiffening.

He'd quite obviously moved closer in his sleep because his conscious mind was horrified.

Hugh didn't want him to feel that way, instead using the moment to get something across to him before everyone else noticed how they were situated. He slid his hand farther onto Adrien's shoulder, keeping him in place as Hugh leaned in and whispered against his ear, "Don't be so alarmed. I quite like you where you are."

Some of the tension in Adrien died down and he peeked up at Hugh's face as if needing to verify with his own eyes the veracity of this claim. Hugh smiled down at him and resisted the urge to kiss Adrien's nose. It wouldn't be appropriate. Damn tempting, though.

Adrien finally relaxed and rolled free. "You are too good-natured, Hugh."

He was not, in fact. This was a different kettle of fish. What was worse, Adrien's normally cognac-smooth voice was raspy from sleep, and it didn't help Hugh's morning wood any. He had to sternly think of man-eating mermaids, aggravating Americans, and other things to calm himself down.

He fed Adrien a plausible excuse for their entanglement, just in case he needed one. "You kept me warm through the night."

"Yes, my cooling charm was a tad overexuberant, wasn't it?" Adrien sat up, a slight smile appearing. "I thought to make it stronger because we had so many men in one area, but perhaps I overdid it."

Cruz spoke up, shaking his blanket out. "No one's complaining, Sorcerer. First time we've been comfortable sleeping on supply run. This charm, can we buy from you?"

"This particular charm is attached to the building," Adrien said apologetically. "But I can fashion one for you that's on a plaque, or something like it, that's portable. You can take it with you as you travel that way."

"I want it. I'll pay for it."

Another crewman—Hugh couldn't remember hearing his name—piped up. "Mosquito charm too."

"I can do both. But first, breakfast. I can craft the charms as we continue down the river."

Even with their frequent stops, it only took two more days to reach their destination. Well, at least to reach the dock that would lead to their destination.

The crew dropped them off at the main dock; they didn't have any intention of lingering, fearful of what lay beyond the tree line. This left Hugh and Adrien to handle their luggage, which admittedly wasn't much since they'd packed light on purpose. With a final wave, the crew wished them best of luck before continuing on to their next drop-off.

The dock was surrounded by thick jungle. From here, Hugh couldn't see his worksite, which was farther into the rainforest. The veritably untouched rainforest, that is. Aside from the villages along the river and the indigenous clans who lived in the area, no one else dared to go this deep. The trees were massive overhead, unchecked by human population, the underbrush thick with shrubs and vines. It smelled of lush earth, plants, humid air, and water. A rich combination of scents and sounds, as all manner of wildlife moved about without care of the two humans in their company. It was deceptively serene.

Adrien had mentioned he would have preferred to create a portal near the docks, in case the situation with the Mapinguari or the Americans proved too volatile, but there was nothing here to anchor a portal to. As expected, they'd have to go farther in to find a doorway.

It was late afternoon now. They were due to check in with Anastasia, but it would have to wait till they had reached the worksite and had an idea of what was going on. Hopefully they would have time to set things up and get the lay of the land before nightfall.

Adrien promptly set up a personal barrier to surround the two of them. "This won't help with the Americans," he said to Hugh, "but it will protect us from anything else trying to attack. Remember, if a Mapinguari ambushes us, aim for the head."

"Roger that."

Adrien shouldered his pack, falling into step with Hugh as they walked along the wooden pathway and toward the rough opening in the tree line. "This pathway seems insufficient for hauling cargo," Adrien said.

"Yes, the infrastructure is one of the many things I'll need to attend to," Hugh said with a resigned sigh, avoiding brushing against the foliage. "Actually, that's what the original crew was for, to clear a pathway and rebuild the docks. Something sturdier than those rickety boards at any—"

In an abrupt move, Adrien threw an arm in front of Hugh's chest, stopping him.

Alert, Hugh put a hand to his gun, going very still. What had Adrien sensed? Hugh strained both ears and eyes but didn't see anything. That meant nothing, of course. The vegetation here was so dense an enemy could be a meter away and Hugh wouldn't have the foggiest clue. Nothing seemed out of the ordinary. The river flowed peacefully behind them, insects and birds flying about, chirping at each other. None of his senses picked up on anything aside from the sticky, hot humidity clinging to his skin and birdsong.

"Something up ahead, in the underbrush," Adrien murmured for his ears alone. "I caught a flash of movement. Where precisely is this village of yours?"

"Just ahead, maybe another five hundred meters. Can we make it?" Hugh would rather not fight anything in this dense jungle.

"I don't—*shite!*"

The foulest scent Hugh had ever had the displeasure of smelling hit him with all the subtlety of a brick to the face. He flinched from it, but he was too seasoned a fighter to simply stand there, his gun quickly drawn and pointed.

Adrien's ward deflected the attack just in time—the creature hit the shield hard, screaming in frustration, then ran again. Disoriented from the scream, Hugh barely got the impression of something much taller than himself, bulky, with matted fur, and that outrageous stench before it disappeared back into the brush.

He gagged, unable to help himself, nearly losing the contents of his stomach. It was a fight to keep his breakfast down. This was with the shield deflecting some of the smell? He couldn't—and didn't want to—imagine what that stench must be like unfiltered.

Adrien didn't seem to be in much better straits, but his hold on Hugh was firm as he urged them forward.

"Go," he choked out. "Go! We can't stand here."

No, they couldn't. It wasn't wise. They were too blocked in; they needed open space and sight lines to stand a prayer. Only the village ahead offered that. Hugh forced himself forward, using his body like a tool, and tried to keep his eyes on their surroundings as they stumbled along the underbrush. Hard to do, as his eyes were watering from the lingering stench in the air.

Truly, nothing he could think of compared to this smell. Rotten potatoes flavored with sweat-soaked socks, stored in an abandoned charnel house, would smell like a perfume compared to this. Adrien's account at the dinner table three nights ago felt like an understatement compared to the reality.

It was a blessing to see the first tip of a thatch roof come into sight. They helped each other the rest of the way in, right onto the remnants of what was likely once a road—the only road really—to the village proper, with its gathering of a dozen or so huts. Sight lines increased and Hugh paused, getting his breath back and feeling better already now that he had clean air passing through his nostrils. He kept his guard up, gun at the ready.

Adrien straightened as well, breathing deeply, and let go of the shields around them. "Hugh, you didn't tell me you had a protective ward up around the village."

He blinked down at the disheveled sorcerer, then looked around. With his eyes no longer full of half-shed tears, that was now obvious. There was a full ward up. "What the devil? I didn't know about this. Wait, why can I see this ward?"

"Most wards are visible as their very presence are to act as a warning. Our last run-in with wards was an outlier due its design to keep something hidden." Adrien gestured to the ward shining overhead. "Something your business partner had done?"

"It would mean getting a sorcerer in here, and we hadn't managed that at all—"

"You didn't, but we did."

Hugh spun, gun up and aimed although he had no idea who he was aiming at. The man coming toward him at a steady walk was dressed like a native, but with that blond hair and fair skin, he was a foreigner to these lands as well. He was also not alone. Several other men approached, all of them with guns trained on Hugh and Adrien.

A grim realization set in. "You're the Americans, I take it. Unfortunate that you're all still alive."

"And you, judging from the accent, must be either Hugh Quartermain or a sorcerer he brought in." The American paused a few feet away, mouth screwed up in something that could be mistaken for a smile. His was a hard face, the look of a man who had done shady dealings all his life, and the mark of it stayed with him.

"I'm Quartermain, yes." Hugh didn't like this at all. He'd been told the Americans had come out here, but he hadn't expected them to still be alive and breathing. Not after what had happened to three of Hugh's work crews. Then again, if the Americans had managed to get a ward up like this, then they had enough magic on their side to thwart the Mapinguari. This ward was much smaller than the barrier that had blocked Hugh from his caves on the Isle of Man, but there had to be at least two sorcerers to keep a rough barrier like this one in place, possibly more.

It meant he and Adrien were outnumbered. Three to one, from the men he saw surrounding them now.

"I don't know what to do with you," the man admitted frankly. "Boss didn't give orders."

"Can't we just kill them?" one of his colleagues asked before spitting tobacco off to the side. "If it's a problem, we can just say the Mapinguari got them before they arrived here."

"We better check first with the boss," the spokesman said. "Just in case. Bill, Jack, grab their weapons."

Hugh groaned as two of the men came in closer and stripped them of packs, Hugh's gun, and what tools Adrien had. They were defenseless now—well, not quite. Hugh held his breath, waiting for someone to check his front pocket. With the bagginess of his cargo pants, it wasn't readily apparent he had something in there.

To his relief, no one checked the pocket. Well now, he'd managed to keep an ace up his sleeve after all. Good. That might turn the tide for them. The men should have had a sorcerer check them over, but Hugh wasn't about to tell them that.

"*Ai'nâahĭ*," Adrien spat as his pack was wrested from his shoulders. "Men's greed should have limits."

Hugh had no idea what the word meant but he agreed with the sentiment wholeheartedly.

"Where do we put them?" Jack or Bill—Hugh hadn't caught who was who—asked. "The hole, maybe?"

"That's a good idea. If one of them's a sorcerer, we can't leave him anywhere with doors or glass, or he'll get them back out again. The hole should keep them just fine."

Hole? Oh, Hugh didn't like the sound of that.

THIRTEEN

Adrien swore roundly, spinning in place as he glanced around the area they'd been dropped into. Casting a mage light, he took in the vertical tunnel, perfectly round along the top and with a flat dirt floor on the bottom—obviously man-made but not a thing in it. Depth was a third the length of a train car, without a single support beam in the whole place. Essentially a well without water, it was literally nothing but stone, dust, and a narrow five-foot-by-five-foot hole leading upward, supposedly for air. Although it smelled very stale down here, so they didn't get much in the way of airflow. Fortunately, they'd been let down with a ladder. It was a good three meters down, which would have made for a difficult landing.

The only good thing about this situation was Adrien hadn't been placed in iron cuffs. They likely hadn't had any lying about, otherwise they'd have certainly used them. Even without the iron cuffs, this was a pickle. He had no way of getting them back out again without getting a bullet to his head for the effort, like a soldier peeking out from the trenches. He'd only been inside this thrice-cursed hole for two minutes and that was plain to see.

The Americans had unfortunately put him in precisely the right place to keep him. With surroundings like these, he couldn't portal them out, as he needed something to anchor the spell to. Something door-ish shaped, and nothing down here remotely sufficed for that. He had no glass—they'd even taken his monocle, curse them!—which meant no way to call for help. The only tool Adrien still had on him was his mithril cuff. The Americans had mistaken it for jewelry and left it on him. Which he was glad for since it was precious to him, but it didn't help get them out of here, either.

The hole was at least inside the ward of the village, so they were safe from attacks from the Mapinguari. That was the only silver lining Adrien could find.

"Well." Hugh gave an exaggerated look around them. "Not quite how I envisioned the day going."

There were times when Adrien blessed the man's easygoing nature, but there were also times when it completely stunned him. Rounding on the man, he took in his thoughtful expression, the relaxed pose, and felt the irrational urge to hit him. "Are you not worried at all?"

"I admit it's a bit troubling," Hugh said with an enigmatic expression, his face awash with shadows from the dim lighting. Was that a smile lurking at the corners of his mouth? "But I do believe they've done me a favor."

Adrien stared at him, nonplussed. "A favor. Pray, explain that one, as I'm quite at sea."

"For the first time since we started this journey"—Hugh approached him in slow, short steps—"I finally have you alone, with no possibility of interruptions, away from any prying eyes. That's a very difficult thing to manage, my dear Adrien. I look at this situation as a gift of sorts."

Adrien could not understand what Hugh meant by that, but he did recognize that the man was serious. There was a very intent look in his eyes.

"I've wanted for some time to confess something to you and could never seem to find the necessary privacy or timing to manage it. It's hardly the right setting, but I think I shall make do. I can't guarantee a situation like this will occur again in the near future."

His words were nonsensical, and Adrien couldn't wrap his head around them. Most likely because he had a hard time focusing on what the man said, attention drawn elsewhere. There was something...something in Hugh's eyes. A deepness, almost a hunger, as he looked at Adrien. He tried to rationalize it away, but his own gut tightened instinctively, his breath quickening. Was that...lust?

Surely not. But...it *looked* like it.

Adrien stood his ground even as Hugh came so close as to encroach on his shadow, feeling his nerves light up with nervous anticipation. No one came this close unless they had a very good reason. Adrien desperately hoped he knew the reason and hadn't read the man wrong. He tilted his head back so he could maintain eye contact with Hugh, voice a tad hoarse. "Was there something you wanted to tell me?"

"Something to say, something to ask," Hugh murmured, closing in the remaining distance slowly, his hand gliding up to cup Adrien's nape. Adrien froze and his lips parted on instinct as the other man pressed in, mouth gentle but insistent, asking for a response. Warm lips pulled gently on his bottom lip, then top, and Adrien groaned, helpless not to respond. He went up on tiptoes, hands grasping Hugh's collar as he leaned in, kissing fervently back. The scent of warm skin filling his head, the brush of stubble against his chin, familiar and unknown at the same time—it was blissful.

Wait. Hugh Quartermain was like him? No, rather, Hugh Quartermain *liked* him?

Retreating a few inches, Hugh drew in quick breaths, a grin taking over his face. "Excellent answer."

For a moment, Adrien was breathless. Pleasure still rocked through his body, lips tingling from that kiss. He'd only fantasized about being held like this by Hugh, and the dream did not begin to compare to reality. Having that strong frame pressed against him, arms securely around Adrien's waist, was both fantasy and delicious reality. He'd never thought this would happen.

He prayed it was not a dream brought on by jungle fever or he'd be quite cross.

Part of Adrien wanted to tug the man about, pin him to the wall, and do perfectly wicked things to him. If they weren't trapped underground with no obvious means of escape, he would have promptly done so. No, bother that, he still needed answers. "What are you even asking me? If I'm attracted to you? A blind man would be attracted, that isn't even a question."

"No," Hugh said patiently, still grinning, his eyes warm with affection. "Although that's quite flattering. I wished to know if you desire me beyond mere attraction. I want you as my lover, Adrien."

Adrien went abruptly still. He couldn't possibly have heard that right.

"You heard me correctly." Hugh's hand came up to brush through Adrien's hair. "Look at you, you're perfectly astonished by this. Have I not made it clear how much I enjoy your company?"

Well, he had, but— "I'm prickly and difficult to deal with. Why would you want me as a lover?"

"This is why I wanted to have the conversation with no

possibility of interruptions," Hugh said, apropos of nothing. "Yes, Adrien, I want you as a lover. I want a relationship with you. I don't find you prickly or difficult, even though you keep telling me you are. But you aren't. Other people have put it into your head that you are, and when I find those stupid people, I will have words with them. Very sharp, pointed words. You are not cold and heartless, especially not with me. You are only ever generous with me."

Well of course he had been. Adrien had done everything in his power to encourage Hugh to stay because he liked the man immensely. As both a person and a friend, not that he'd ever seriously entertained the idea of having Hugh as something beyond a friend. Adrien felt completely at a loss for words; he didn't know how to respond to this confession. No, he did know how he wanted to respond, he just didn't know how wise it would be.

"Adrien." Hugh whispered another kiss against his mouth, so gentle and sweet it stole Adrien's breath. "I want you. A lover, a friend, a confidant—I want all of that with you."

"Yes," Adrien burst out, completely without planning to. His emotions overcame his rational mind for a split second, the blood rushing to his head in a dizzying manner. "All of that, yes."

Lighting up in incandescent joy, Hugh leaned in to kiss him senseless. Adrien tried to kiss him back just as fervently, but the man had quite effectively shut his mind off, and Adrien found himself swept along for the ride instead.

They lingered over the kiss once, twice, a third time before Hugh retreated the barest distance, giving them both a chance to catch their breath. Adrien's mouth felt damp and a little used, pleasantly so, as his body remembered the pleasure it took in a good snog. He tried to keep his face from doing something strange, but he had a feeling his grin came out more than a smidge demented. "You brilliant nutter. Why you would choose to confess down here, where we don't even have a bed on hand, is beyond me."

"I told you, it's deucedly difficult to get you alone. I promise we'll spend more time with each other, in every sense, but later. Now that we have this sorted, I suppose we can work on escaping."

"Oh, you suppose so, do you?" Adrien rolled his eyes in exasperation. "Hugh, in case it has escaped your immediate notice, I have no means of working magic on me except willpower.

Every spell I could use to either portal us out or contact help is unavailable to me. If I try to fight my way out—and I hesitate to do so under these circumstances—then we'll be a sitting target. They've been fiendishly clever in trapping me down here."

"Yes, quite clever with *you*," Hugh said with that wicked gleam Adrien recognized. It always prefaced something brilliant on Hugh's part. "But did you notice that after they took my revolver away from me, they failed to search the rest of my person?"

Adrien looked up at him sharply. "What do you have?"

Grinning, Hugh said cheerfully, "All manner of things, really. I created a case to keep certain items on me when I'm out with you. I reckoned they'd come in handy eventually." From his front cargo pocket, he pulled free something that looked like a cigar case, although longer than average. He opened the silver case and displayed the interior of it for Adrien's perusal.

His gaze flickered over the contents, taking stock, eyebrows climbing slowly into his hairline. Inside was a small round mirror, latched to the interior of the case—something that would fit inside a woman's compact. Four small rods that looked like collapsed antennas, a length of twine, and a thick piece of chalk. In fact, in this case alone, Hugh had managed to gather every element Adrien needed to either call for help or portal them out altogether. It was stunningly well thought out and Adrien felt fit to burst with pride for the man.

Unable to help himself, he seized Hugh's face with both hands and planted a sound kiss on his lips. "You are the most ingenious man in all of Britain."

Chuckling, Hugh handed him the case. "Glad you think so, dearest."

Adrien took it and pulled out the antennas, finding them only to be three feet in length, hardly enough to go on with, but tall enough that they should be able to crawl through. "However did you think of these?"

"Do you remember that conversation we had before breaching the barrier at the caves, when you were explaining to me that anything could be used to form a rough doorway for you to anchor a portal spell to? That's when the idea came to me. I had to craft these myself, as most of what's available on the market didn't have the right size to be portable. The twine's there to help tie it all together." Hugh shrugged as if this were no major feat. "And the mirror, of course, that seemed an obvious choice to me. You and Julian are forever using mirrors or panes of glass to call people, so why not carry something on me, just in case?"

"Brilliant." The Americans' first mistake was in assuming Hugh Quartermain didn't pay attention. He was an engineer, a genius in his field, but no one seemed to look at the man and really *comprehend* that. Sometimes not even Adrien. Of course he would observe Adrien work, his busy mind absorbing facts and turning them end over end, coming up with its own conclusions. Adrien quite gleefully promised himself he'd rub the mistake in his enemies' faces with a handful of salt and lye to boot.

Hugh knelt to help him put the antennas together in a rough square, something resembling a doorway, and it was very squat indeed but it would suffice. Adrien chose not to use it immediately, needing to ascertain where it would be safe to portal out to. Lifting the mirror, he invoked the spell, calling Julian.

"*Master! Thank heavens. I tried calling but couldn't reach you!*"

"As to that, we've had a bit of an unpleasant turn here. Julian, you and MacMallin are all right?"

"*Yes, of course. Why, what's happened?*"

"I'll explain when I see you. Where are you, then? The hotel?"

"*Yes. Can you tell us where you are?*"

"It won't do any good, I'm afraid, but due to Hugh's cleverness, we have the means for me to portal us out. Stand back from the door, we're coming through shortly." Adrien ended the connection, replacing the mirror back in the case. There was one more question he needed to ask before they escaped. As he handed the case to Hugh, he asked hesitantly, "How...discreet do you need us to be?"

Hugh met his eyes levelly. "My mother, business partners, master, and a few select friends know my nature. I've no need to hide from them. You?"

"Everyone in my inner circle, who you've basically met, knows about me. My sister's and cousin's family as well. I've no need to hide anything from them either." Tentatively, he said in reluctant tones, "Except possibly my sister. I can tell her things, but I'm not sure how far her tolerance extends."

"But you see her rarely, correct?" Hugh paused, waited for his nod, then gave him a bracing smile. "Then that's fine. We'll be discreet in public but as affectionate as we wish with friends and family."

That sounded a jolly sight better than any other offer Adrien had ever been handed. He stole another kiss, smiled at Hugh, and resisted the urge to go for more. But he really wanted out of this blasted hole, so he focused on their makeshift doorway, relieved when the spell anchored well enough to give them a perfectly clear view of the hotel room. "After you. And be sure to not jostle the sides."

Nodding, Hugh crawled through on hands and knees, careful with his elbow placement and wider frame. Extinguishing his mage light, Adrien quickly followed on his heels, relieved when his palms and knees met tiled flooring instead of packed earth.

Two sets of hands grabbed him under the arms and hoisted him up, MacMallin on one side, Julian on the other, and he barely had his feet under him when both boys enfolded him into a group hug. Relieved, he hugged them back, eyes closing as he took a moment and appreciated that he and Hugh had come through safely despite the odds. Captain circled them, poking at Adrien's thighs with his nose, inquiring if all was well. He spared a good scratch behind the ears to reassure the dog.

"Adrien, what the devil?" Anastasia asked in alarm, her eyes on the doorway. She was in her work dress, an all-black lehenga choli, her inky black hair done up in a smart bun, indicating she'd been in the middle of something when their call had come through. "Why are you crawling through—is that a hole you were in?"

"Unfortunately."

"If you're going to get yourself into trouble, warn me first!"

"If my enemies will kindly warn me as well, I'll be happy to," he promised sardonically. "Wait, I want to do a quick retrieval spell."

Hugh cottoned on to his meaning, glancing toward the open portal. "I can make others, you know, unless you wish to confound the Americans?"

"More the latter. Besides, if we have a method of keeping a means of escape on us, I'd prefer to keep that card up our metaphorical sleeve. It'll make future troubles easier to navigate."

"Seems wise," Hugh said.

Adrien bent to it. It was tricky, retrieving the very thing a portal spell anchored to; he had to be quicker than the portal spell's collapse. But it wasn't like he hadn't done this once or twice before. He spoke the spell, tugged hard, and caught the three antennas handily like an acrobat catching a thrown knife.

Hugh took them to undo the twine and collapse them down. Of course it drew MacMallin's attention, and after a moment, Julian's, and both boys came in closer for a better look.

"I quite like the assortment in that case, sir," Julian said, blue eyes glued on the interior.

"I'll make you one," Hugh said with a smile. "As we just learned, it comes in handy."

Adrien's concern was on something else. The boys normally only called when there was trouble. "You said you were trying to reach us, Julian. Why?"

Julian blinked at him and then straightened abruptly. "It's not good news, sir."

"Let's sit." Anastasia waved to the small sitting area off to the side of the entryway.

Adrien brushed his knees off before going to the settee, sitting there with an aggravated groan. Of course something else had gone wrong today. It seemed the day for it. He still mentally kicked himself for dropping his guard just because he'd come inside the village's ward. He shouldn't have assumed that it automatically meant safety.

In the future, he would not be so careless.

Hugh settled in next to him, sitting close enough their thighs pressed together. Anastasia took the chair to the side and the boys sat on the couch opposite. Adrien could see signs they had been studying before the interruption. Books and papers were all over the coffee table, along with water glasses. Captain promptly sat on Hugh's feet, tail wagging happily. The collie had everyone herded into one space, so he was quite pleased with himself.

"While you were out, the boys and I managed to find out who the Americans are. A company called Caddel is here. They're determined to overtake the manganese mines."

"However did you learn this?" Hugh asked.

Anastasia rolled her eyes. "The group was quite stupid about it. I don't know why men think that just because they're in a foreign country, no one can understand what they're saying if they speak in English. I think they overlooked me, and I walked right past them in a marketplace and heard them talking. I pretended to look at some fabric—bought some, too, it's very pretty—and listened for several minutes. Their boss is aware that you're here, Hugh, and he's determined to thwart you."

The company name didn't mean anything to Adrien, but it apparently did to Hugh. He had the air of a man who was utterly done. Adrien nudged him with his elbow. "Who is it?"

"Patrick Caddel is one of the more ruthless, enterprising American tycoons of my acquaintance." Hugh rubbed his forehead with a sigh. "Really, when I heard Americans were here, he should have been my first guess. He and I are in the same line of business, and we often clash like this when reaching for resources. I believe this makes it the sixth time. Granted, it's usually not on this scale."

Anastasia asked the obvious question. "What are the odds you can peacefully negotiate him into leaving?"

"I'd have better luck convincing a bear to dance."

Well that was a blunt answer. Adrien resigned himself to doing this the hard way. "We're going to have to fight them out and then erect multiple wards to keep them out. Aren't we?"

"I'm afraid so. I'm very glad now that you've asked Cynric to come. We've a fight on our hands."

Yes, Adrien was quite glad of that too. All said, it did mean something else had to change. "Anastasia, I think it goes without saying, it's not safe for you or the boys here. Please portal all of you away from here."

She nodded, not surprised. "I thought you'd say that. It's why I stayed mostly packed. I asked about, found a lovely little beach house much farther south from here, so we'll portal there for the time being. If it's safe to come back, we will. I'd rather not portal overseas with the boys if I can help it."

"I frankly don't blame you." Adrien wouldn't want to in her shoes.

"I did bring a healthy amount of mithril with me, just in case. I've rested up enough to make the consecutive portaling easy for the short distance, but I'll need a bit longer to store enough magic to portal overseas with the boys."

The boys looked resigned and not entirely happy about the decision, but Adrien could not risk them. If anyone made the connection of who they were to Hugh, they'd likely be taken as hostages. It was better to not even entertain the possibility.

"But as a consolation prize..." Hugh slid his hand into Adrien's and lifted it to kiss the knuckles, blue eyes warm with affection. "I have convinced him to date."

"Convinced" was such a ridiculous word to use. All he'd had to do was ask before Adrien had blurted out "yes."

All three let out a cheer and clapped, which was ridiculous, but it made Adrien laugh. Also strangely shy.

"If you being alone together on the river resulted in this, I can't be mad anymore at being left behind." MacMallin gave them a cheeky wink. "Glad to see this."

"So am I." Anastasia put a hand over her heart. "I thought you two would never stop dancing around each other. Well, I'm not in the mood to linger here to no purpose. Boys, pack up. Let's be gone within the hour. Adrien, Hugh, I don't have to tell you two to wait on Cynric before going back into the rainforest, do I?"

"It won't be only Cynric we'll take back in," Hugh promised her. "I'll rally a fighting force before we attempt this again."

"Good. I knew you had some common sense. Just don't die. I don't want to clean up after you."

It was said with such love that Adrien shook his head, chuckling. "Noted, Anastasia. We'll do our best."

FOURTEEN

Anastasia was true to her word. She and the boys and Captain left within the hour. With everything that had happened today, Adrien wasn't in the mood to be social downstairs. He wanted time with Hugh without prying eyes. They ordered room service up to Adrien's room instead, ate heartily, and then returned the dishes on the cart to the hallway with a Do Not Disturb sign hanging on the door handle.

Adrien didn't know if it was too soon to ask for this. Frankly, he'd not attempted a real relationship with someone since he was twenty. He just wanted to touch Hugh. Adrien felt like they'd been dancing about each other ever since they'd boarded the boat for Brazil, really—those little touches all fanning the flames for this moment.

Hugh seemed of the same mind. He took one of Adrien's hands in his, eyes intent. "It's quite all right if you're not in the mood for more, but...will you stay with me tonight?"

Adrien almost blurted out another "yes" but managed to catch it behind his teeth this time. Being too eager had never done him any good. Instead, he gripped that hand in his, playing with the calloused fingers, trying to suppress a goofy smile before it escaped.

"I'd like that very much." He peeked up through his lashes, saw blatant hunger in Hugh's eyes, and swallowed hard. The man might eat him whole at this rate.

Adrien couldn't wait to be back in his arms but couldn't help it as past trauma tried to rear its head. Nerves strung tight, he ruthlessly forced it away, as such thoughts had no business between him and Hugh. Especially not on their first night together. This was what truly mattered. He wanted—craved—Hugh more than anything.

Perhaps Hugh sensed his nerves. Perhaps he felt something

of the same. His hands were gentle as they drew Adrien into him, shifting to a light hold around his waist.

Adrien came easily, hands touching Hugh's warm, broad chest before sliding up. His mouth parted as Hugh bent, their lips finding each other. Hugh's were so soft, fitting against Adrien's like they were made for this. Hot breath, the taste of skin—it wiped all thought from Adrien's head.

More.

Hugh caught Adrien's bottom lip between his lips. He tugged it into his mouth to worry it before pulling free, just enough to change angles and dive back in. Kissing the man was pure bliss, every second of it satisfying—and yet it drew a responding hunger from within Adrien. He needed more contact with Hugh. He wanted to shed clothes, feel the caress of hot skin against his own. He wanted to feel the full pressure of Hugh's weight against him as he gave himself to this man.

Adrien hadn't felt this nervous since his first lover, many years ago now. He'd thought he was past this feeling entirely, but the butterflies in his stomach were more like rhinos engaging in a bout of fisticuffs. He'd only attempted to bed a fellow European twice in his life—both times ending rather disastrously. He'd learned quickly that there was a great deal of nonsense and prejudices regarding two men engaged in intercourse, none of it making any sense to him. But offering to take a submissive role had gotten him quickly scorned, and the memories still burned in the back of his mind.

What he wanted…was probably something he shouldn't ask for. Part of him was convinced that if he did, Hugh would never look at him the same. But the other part, the one that said he could trust the man, urged him to ask. A devil and an angel on the shoulder, respectively.

Hugh sensed his nerves and his kiss gentled, sweetened, the urgency in his touch abating as he withdrew a little. He touched their foreheads together, breaths mingling in quick pants. "My dear Adrien. Is this your first time with a man?"

"No." Adrien tried to force his nerves to stay out of his voice. "It's not that."

"Ah." A wealth of understanding filled Hugh's tone. "I assure you, I won't demand anything you're uncomfortable with."

"That's good to hear—and the reverse is equally true, I promise you—but...what I'm trying to convey is..." Dammit, why was this so hard to frame into words?

"Is...?" Hugh asked, encouraging him gently.

In a split second, Adrien decided to the devil with it. He'd trust first, doubt later. "I want you to take me."

"With pleasure," Hugh rumbled, practically purring. He kissed Adrien again, demanding now, the urgency returning.

Adrien flowed into the kiss, melting with relief. That had gone so much better than he'd feared. Then again, he shouldn't be surprised. Hugh wasn't the kind of man to scorn another based on silly conceptions, was he? The thought made him smile even as he wrestled with the man's belt.

Lifting his head up a little, Hugh muttered, "Surely you've a spell to get us unclothed faster."

Arching an eyebrow, Adrien said, *"Campa le nix."*

In an instant, all clothes were whisked off and flung onto a chair nearby. Hugh startled visibly, watched their route, then a wicked smile broke over his face. "Having a sorcerer for a lover certainly has its advantages."

That it did, and Adrien was reaping the benefits already. He'd not seen Hugh without clothing before, of course, and it was a damn shame. Such a fine view shouldn't be covered all the time. Hugh's strength was apparent in his biceps, his chest—not harshly defined but smooth and eminently touchable. His ginger hair covered his chest in a light sprinkling, leading down into a happy trail Adrien really wanted to put his mouth on. All that creamy skin was his for the taking, his mind going straight into the gutter about what he'd do to this man.

In a husky tone, Hugh murmured, "Now. There's a little something I want to try."

Adrien rather lost the thread as the man was kissing and sucking his way along Adrien's jaw and down his neck. It felt insanely lovely to have hot, naked skin pressed along his, to feel the crinkle of chest hair brush along him. His hands kept wandering along Hugh's back and thighs, wanting to deepen the contact and relish it at the same time.

Hugh pushed them back, toward the bed, only pausing in his caresses until he could get Adrien up onto the bed. Then he crawled back onto him, his weight half on top of Adrien's. The heaviness was more than welcome, and Adrien smiled, his hands doing their best to hold Hugh there.

When Hugh's tongue dipped into his navel, he lifted his head up to watch, body tingling with anticipation. Would he be licked there as well? Would Hugh take him into his mouth and—Adrien's hands gripped at the sheets, pulling them taut as a warm mouth wrapped around the head of his cock and sucked lightly. God, that felt good. Adrien tipped his head back, eyes sliding closed in pleasure.

"You're incredibly good at that," he murmured, untangling a hand from the sheets to stroke through that thick copper hair.

Hugh hummed around him; an answer, perhaps, or just teasing. Adrien enjoyed the vibrations regardless, and when Hugh moved to put both of Adrien's legs over his shoulders, he didn't think anything of it. He continued to just enjoy, fully planning to return the favor, as Hugh's lips and tongue moved over his balls, massaging them in a wet glide.

Then his mouth went even lower, and Adrien's eyes popped open. He wasn't—was he? Adrien had heard of this but never bedded anyone interested in doing it. Or who would even contemplate doing it. Adrien barely had the gumption to ask someone to top him, much less anything more intimate, and this was decidedly more intimate. "H-Hugh?"

"Have you tried this?" Hugh whispered against his skin before grazing his teeth against the side of Adrien's thigh.

"I—that is, no, no one's ever been willing to. Have you?"

"Yes, twice before. It was immensely pleasurable. Tell me if you wish for me to stop."

At the first swipe of Hugh's tongue against his entrance, the furthest thing from Adrien's mind was requesting Hugh to stop. It felt nice; a little strange, but quite enjoyable. Hugh grasped his thighs, turning him and changing the angle, and it stopped being *nice* and became something far more intense. Adrien scrambled for the sheets, the pillow, anything that came to hand as his body tensed and shuddered, nerves alight with fire. God above, that was...words failed to describe it.

"Ai'Hugh," he gasped, shuddering under the man's hands and mouth, body arching as it desperately sought more of the touch. "Ai'Hugh—please—"

He wasn't even sure what he was pleading for, what he needed. Something. Anything, really, to relieve some of the tension of his overstimulated nerves.

A blunt, thick finger breached him, gliding gently in and out, and that was better. It gave him the feeling he craved. But it also stimulated him in a wholly different manner, threatening to topple him over entirely. Adrien's back arched, and a whine caught in the back of his throat. He was making perfectly embarrassing sounds, he knew he was, but couldn't seem to cage them.

When a second finger joined the first, stretching him, he fell to sporadic chanting and demands. "Hugh, in me. In me, please. Hugh. Ai'Hugh!"

Hugh gently lowered him, and he was for a split second quite upset at that. It was his ears picking up the sound of a glass jar that kept him from protesting. The vial of oil, of course. That was what Hugh needed. Where he'd gotten it was a question for later, as Adrien only cared about its existence right then. Adrien turned, caught some of the oil spilling over into Hugh's hand, and dropped his fingers to Hugh's length. Hugh's lips parted, eyes closing to half-mast as he thrust into Adrien's hand.

"That's good, *mo ghràidh*," he encouraged, voice rough with passion. "I want to take you from behind."

"God, yes." Adrien agreed without thinking. He let go—a little regretfully, as he enjoyed having that thick, hard length in his hand—and turned again, intending to get up on hands and knees.

"No." Hugh caught him around the waist and drew him back down. "Here, side by side, like this."

Adrien had never been in this position before and wasn't sure what to think of it. Then Hugh lay down behind him, his chest against Adrien's back, and he thought he rather might like it after all. It would certainly ensure they'd be pressed up against each other. Adrien secretly liked the idea of being held even as he was taken.

Hugh's blunt tip breached him, and he slowly but steadily slid his way in. Adrien sighed and moved into it, as much as he was able. It burned some, but he liked the burn of penetration. Hugh felt hard and hot inside of him, like a brand, and that was immensely pleasurable as well. Adrien grasped the back of the man's thigh, pulling him in tighter.

Hugh bottomed out, then stopped, breath shaking against Adrien's nape. "You feel so...dammit. All right?"

"I'll be a sight better than that when you start moving."

What might have been a chuckle passed the man's lips, then Hugh drew back an inch before thrusting in again. Adrien arched into it, eyes slipping closed. Yes, perfect. This was all so beautifully perfect. Lying here in Hugh's arms, having the man pressed up against his back even as they were wrapped in each other's pleasure. Adrien wanted to bottle this moment, preserve it somehow, and his heart ached with the realization that he couldn't.

Hugh tipped his head to the side so that he could set lips to Adrien's neck, and he allowed this, wanting Hugh to brand him, even if it was transient in the extreme. As he sucked on Adrien's skin, Hugh slid a hand around his stomach and gathered up his hard cock that was weeping for attention. Adrien let out a hoarse shout of relief as Hugh's hand stroked him in time with the thrusts.

Adrien's climax was building; he could feel the tingle and tension of it in his groin, and he wanted to hold on to it. But his body was a selfish thing, demanding release, and Hugh seemed intent on driving him over the edge. He let himself indulge, climaxing over Hugh's hand and his own stomach. Adrien's vision went dark, and he lay gasping for breath, riding the wave of endorphins with a smile on his face.

Clasping him tightly, Hugh drove into him with more force, seeking and finding his own climax a short time later. It was a bit much for Adrien's sensitized body, but he uttered not a word of complaint, as he liked this, too. The warm spread of Hugh's semen filled Adrien's channel before Hugh abruptly relaxed against his back, sighing gustily.

Not wishing to be sticky, Adrien muttered a spell with a wave, cleaning them both up. He had no other urges to move, and lay content in his lover's arms. Hugh seemed of the same mind, as they basked in the afterglow without a word being passed between them. Settled like this, skin to skin, with their bodies still roused from recent exertions, Adrien felt on the verge of being too hot. But even that seemed an indulgence, so he kept quiet, enjoying the press of their bodies together.

"Thank you," Hugh finally whispered against his neck. "I know how much courage this takes, to trust another man as you just did me."

Adrien lifted Hugh's hand to his face, kissing the palm before cradling it to his own chest. "You've always given me every reason to trust you. I decided to bank on that."

"I'm glad you did. Should I pull out?"

"No, stay." Adrien meant to sound confident, but the words were a little shy as he admitted, "I enjoy the sensation."

"Ah. Well, I enjoy being connected with you in such a way, so in truth I'm in no hurry to move." Hugh tried, impossibly, to pull him in a little tighter. "Adrien, at some point we need to discuss how to move forward."

Practical man that he was, this didn't surprise Adrien. "I agree."

"I don't..." Adrien heard Hugh's intake of breath. "I don't want to give you the idea that I want something casual or transient with you."

Adrien found himself holding his breath, as if even breathing might disturb this moment. He hadn't really thought that—Hugh wasn't the type for casual sex—but...what was he leading up to?

"To that end, I must tell you first that I'm very much in love with you."

Adrien froze, listening to that warm voice as it traced words upon his skin. Those words had an electrifying effect on Adrien's heart; he both soared and reeled under the realization. This incredible man was in love with him? How in the devil had Adrien secured his affections? "You are?"

"This surprises you?"

"A little. In the hole, before, you spoke openly of your desires and I knew that you liked me but...well." A cynical smile traced its way onto his lips. "Desire and affection often don't share the same bed, in my experience." Feeling he should be equally candid, he whispered, "I'm falling quite head over heels for you too, my darling."

Hugh kissed his bare shoulder. "I'm joyously happy to hear it. And relieved. You're not an easy man to win over."

Adrien snorted. "I'm aware. The path ahead of us won't be easy, though, Hugh."

"I know. Which is why we have to sit and properly discuss how to walk that path. I'll not lose you because we failed to think ahead."

His lover was indeed diligent through and through. The realization made Adrien smile. "I agree. I've a few ideas in mind of how to make it easy for us to see each other discreetly."

"Oh? I'll be eager to hear them." Hugh's head dropped to the crook of Adrien's neck and stayed there.

Adrien sensed his lover perhaps needed a moment. The confession alone was enough to warrant that, much less their becoming lovers. For that matter, he needed one too, as part of his mind was still reeling. Hugh was in love with him. Adrien felt rather the cad for not properly facing the man before today. If he'd possessed any idea that accepting Hugh would lead to this, he'd have gathered up the proper courage well before now. Knowing he had this man's heart was elating but also terrifying. He never, ever wanted to break it, but feared he might.

"Here, let me pull out. We need to properly get situated and talk." Hugh pulled free with a huff.

Adrien concealed a wince, as that did smart more than he'd expected. Then again, it had been many months since he'd indulged himself in such a way. Perhaps a balm was in order. Adrien had full plans to indulge again later, and by later he did not mean tomorrow.

They rearranged pillows, propping up a little to speak easier, Hugh once again snuggling Adrien into his arms. Adrien strongly suspected Hugh was a cuddler. It was strange to have a lover who was. Adrien himself was not…shall we say, touchy by nature. But he did enjoy the intimacy. The way Hugh touched him made Adrien feel cherished.

Adrien leaned up to steal a kiss, then another, wanting to taste Hugh's smile. He was very invested in keeping that smile on Hugh's face. "I've two notions that will help us see each other readily. The first is simple. I can create a permanent portal between your house and my flat, something we can both use at will."

A blink, and the wheels started to clearly turn in Hugh's mind. "You said long-distance portals are draining and that holding spells took significant energy, though. Won't this be problematic?"

"In the normal sense, you're correct. But with the proper design, it won't be a spell I hold. Think of it more like one of your machines. Once created, and with the appropriate power source, it'll run on its own."

"Ah. Power source?"

"Well, since I have a healthy supply of mithril," Adrien said dryly, "I thought to use it."

Hugh's eyes crinkled up at the corners. "You may have as much as your heart desires. I'm very satisfied with this idea. Let's attend to it when we're back home. What is your second notion?"

"This one will take a few hours on my part to develop, but there is a way to create a talisman that will link to another. It will operate much like a telephone. That way we can be constantly in contact without anyone the wiser."

Hugh slow blinked as he took in the idea. "A talisman. Truly?"

"It's what sorcerers used to use, before telephones became all the rage," Adrien said with a casual shrug of one shoulder. "It can be anything. A watch, earring, necklace, pocket watch—it works better if attached to metals. Well, aside from iron, of course. Platinum especially has the right magical resonance for it."

"I hesitate to have a ring," Hugh said, still thinking hard judging by the furrow in his brow. "Engineers, you know, our hands are constantly in the belly of machinery. I saw a man lose a finger once because of a wedding ring."

"By Jove!" Adrien said in horror. "Then no, I veto that option strongly. I like your hands as they are."

"I do as well. A necklace?"

"If that's your wish, by all means. I might opt for a ring, myself. I am appallingly bad about having anything restrictive about my neck. The talismans don't have to match each other in type, just in design of purpose."

Hugh's eyes were warm and somehow amused as he regarded Adrien steadily. "You're telling me that somehow, during the course of everything that happened today, you've found a moment to think about portals and talismans?"

Adrien almost blithely derailed him, but instinct held the words in check. Hugh was so open with him, after all, and hadn't he just learned that he could trust his lover? Still, it was embarrassing to admit and a flush heated his cheeks, his eyes skittering off as he said, "A man's allowed to fantasize, isn't he?"

A soft, soundless laugh shook Hugh's chest as he hugged Adrien to him, kissing the top of his head. "I adore you. You've fantasized about us to the point you've worked out all the logistics?"

"I overthink things," Adrien said, still embarrassed, but not enough to refuse the embrace.

"By all means, love, do so if it means dreaming of how we can be together. I admit to thinking about things as well. I want to tell you, without fear, that I love you. I realize doing so aloud or even in a written word might draw unwanted attention, though."

How true. Adrien already felt himself chafing at the restriction, but he felt like Hugh had a plan in mind. "So what is your idea?"

Hugh didn't respond verbally. He tapped a finger to Adrien's skin, a quick, light staccato of three. "Three taps mean I love you. Or three gentle squeezes."

Oh. How beautifully simple and easily something that they could both do in public without anyone the wiser. Adrien immediately tapped a finger lightly to Hugh's chest three times.

Hugh responded with three gentle squeezes against his upper arm.

"I think," Hugh murmured, "that I will be saying those words to you rather often."

Adrien drew him back in for a kiss, his finger tapping three times on Hugh's chest even as their lips met. He felt Hugh smile into the kiss because of it.

Hugh wasn't the only one who would say it often.

FIFTEEN

The next morning, Adrien barely had pants and shirt on when there was a knock at the door. If it was possible for a knock to sound aggrieved, this one managed it. He checked only to see if Hugh was decent enough for company—he was—before answering.

On the other side, looking rather a mix between peeved and suspicious, stood Cynric. He had a suitcase in one hand, his weapons case hanging over the other shoulder, and the look of a man who had just finished one job before portaling right to Brazil. He likely had. His thick black hair was ruffled, khaki pants and shirt looking slept in, and somehow his olive skin looked even darker. Had he been living outdoors the past few weeks?

"You," Cynric said, "are trouble. Sis told me you had to escape from Americans? Really, Adrien, Americans?"

"Come in." Adrien invited him in as if they were exchanging pleasantries. "We just ordered breakfast up. Do put all that down and sit for a spell."

Cynric did so, spotting Hugh seated at the small round table in front of the window as he came inside, and did a double take. Then his eyes went back to Adrien, studying him quickly from head to toe and back again, before his dark brown eyes flared wide with awareness.

That expression said it all. Anastasia had not stolen Adrien's thunder and told her brother about Adrien's personal status changing. Just Hugh being in his room at this hour of the morning, barely dressed in pants and shirt, would have suggested something going on. Adrien was aware he had love marks on his neck, his hair uncombed as of yet. It must be obvious in a glance that he'd spent most of the evening and night making love with Hugh.

A delighted smile lit up Cynric's face. "You didn't."

"I assure you, I did," Adrien drawled, tone very satisfied.

"You did," he said, beaming now. "Ha! Well done, Hugh. I

knew I could trust you."

Hugh chuckled, eyes sparkling. "Thank you."

"Well. Now I'm not nearly as upset after hearing this. You two finally got your heads out of your arses. I guess getting thrown into a hole was worth it."

Adrien would have loved to make some wisecrack denying this…but it happened to be true. He still had no idea what Hugh had been thinking when confessing to him down there. It was the most unromantic spot possible. He sighed in aggravation instead and prodded Cynric toward the table.

Cynric chuckled like a demented drunk, put his luggage down next to the door, and joined them at the table, still smiling all the while. He'd be insufferable the rest of the day. Adrien could see it now.

Breakfast arrived, fortunately in a sufficient serving to feed Cynric as well, once another set of cutlery and china was brought up. They settled in to eat. The coffee was especially welcome. Adrien didn't regret one second of last night, but it had left him short on sleep, and he felt the lack of it this morning.

Cynric looked rather more restored too after eating. He glanced between them as he asked, "Catch me up? Stacey only said something about Americans also being on site with the Mapinguari. How many? Can we force them out legally?"

Hugh fielded the questions with a grimace. "My business partner has already attempted the legal route. The American Embassy doesn't care. There's no mayor in charge of the Amazon Rainforest itself, so anything short of federal interference on my behalf won't budge them. It's rather a lawless place in that sense. I do have the rights to mine there, obtained federally, so they are clearly poaching. But what we were told, in no uncertain terms, was that this was our problem to deal with."

"So anything goes?" Cynric shrugged. "All right. Makes it easier on us, I suppose. Kill everything."

"Unfortunately, it'll come to that." Adrien sipped his coffee. "And then spend the next three days warding everything to keep them out."

"I kill, you ward?" Cynric offered.

"There's enough of them I'll have to help you. They've at least two sorcerers there. But yes, in essence, that's how this job will break down. Also, Cyn, I can confirm the Mapinguari are right in that area. We encountered one just walking up from the river."

Cynric drank his coffee and made a face. "I find no joy in this knowledge."

"I can't disagree. Still, brace yourself. The one advantage we have is that the Americans managed to get a ward up over the village."

Cynric's dark brows rose. "Oh-ho. Did they now? That gives us a safe place to retreat to. They kept the ward open for future workers, I take it."

"That's my guess. Hence why we were able to walk inside of it. I think it was only created to keep the local predators out."

"Makes sense." Cynric set his coffee down with a soft clink. "All right, so here's my take on how this will go. We go in with a fighting force, wipe out anyone who's there, then use the ward they have up as a station to deal with the Mapinguari. God, I have the most sour taste in my mouth saying that. I hate Mapinguari."

Just the memory of the smell alone was enough to make Adrien nauseous, so he agreed with his friend. "I'm not pleased with them either, but they must be dealt with. After we're certain we've killed them, then we take over the ward and start adjusting. Well, I can, you can return home at that point if you'd like."

Hugh lifted a finger in question. "You keep saying 'they' when you refer to the Mapinguari. Are you so sure that there's more than one in the area?"

"Mapinguari move in mated pairs," Cynric said. "They're rather territorial even with themselves, so they don't tend to live in, like, clans or anything. They move about as young ones just enough to meet other Mapinguari, mate, and then find a new unclaimed territory to settle in. That's why if you see one in an area, odds are very high there's a second one somewhere."

"Ah." Hugh made a face. "Just one's bad enough."

"None of us like battling two, but at least it's not more than two. Silver lining." Cynric shrugged, resigned on this point. "All right, how do you propose we go in? You said you walked in from the river, so you took a boat in? Why?"

"I didn't know what the situation was there," Adrien said patiently. "I didn't want to pop in and assume we were safe. I had the naïve thought that I could create a ward and a permanent portal so we could bring you in and have an escape route ready."

Cynric canted his head back and forth. "I can't fault the logic.

This time, let's just portal in. I don't think it'll be any safer to travel by boat, for one thing, and that way we have more of an element of surprise. If the ward is so lax that it lets anyone pass through, then they won't have it blocked against portaling."

"The situation might have changed," Adrien said with a shake of his head. It was a thought that had plagued him this morning as he dressed. "We disappeared out of a hole without any sign. A hole that was inside the ward, so it's not like a predator got to us. They may have tightened up security because of it."

"Ah. Damn, good point. Well, I suppose all we can do is try. We'll default to boat if we have to."

"Either way, I'll create personal shields for everyone before going in. I don't want to lose anyone just because I failed to prepare them properly for it." Which did beg the question. Adrien turned to his lover and asked, "How many men will you bring in with us?"

"My hope is a dozen. I'll need to confer with people, make some inquiries this morning, before I can give you a firm number."

A dozen, eh? Well, a dozen should be fine with Cynric in the mix. He fought like four people anyway.

Adrien handed Cynric the room key for next door—what had been Anastasia's room—so he could freshen up and sleep for a few hours. It wasn't like they were going to launch into action this morning. They needed at least today to prepare before going in. Perhaps tomorrow too.

With Cynric gone, Adrien finished dressing for the day. Or at least, he attempted to, but the second he lifted a comb, two strong arms wrapped around his waist and snuggled him into a firm chest.

Laughing softly, he indulged Hugh, sinking into his arms and relaxing.

"You make me happy, you know."

Shouldn't that be Adrien's line? "I do?"

Hugh spoke in a low, almost raspy voice against his temple. "The way you unapologetically tell people we're in a relationship warms me in ways that I can't convey. I've never had a lover like you, who faces the world and lets the chips fall where they may. I'm in no doubt where I stand with you, and I appreciate it very much."

For all that Adrien had a very shitty dating history, apparently Hugh's wasn't perfect either. He didn't seem traumatized by past lovers, at least. Just hadn't had the best of luck with communication. Adrien would've liked to ask more questions, but this wasn't the time for it.

"I don't want to be in that state of uncertainty with you. I know we have to be discreet in public, the backlash and legal consequences aren't something either of us wants, but among our own circle? I won't pretend we're anything else."

Hugh kissed his forehead and gave a content sigh. "You really are a genius at making me happy."

This man was far too easy to please. Adrien snorted but he smiled, too. He wasn't confident in making anyone happy in a relationship, so hearing that he was already off on a good footing with Hugh? Very good news indeed.

On that note, he asked, "Hugh, is there a place to buy raw metal around here?"

"I'm sure there is. Why?"

"Before we go back into the rainforest, I want to craft the necklace and ring we spoke of last night. I plan on being at your side at every moment in the fight, but just in case we are separated for whatever reason, I want to be able to contact you." Adrien turned in his arms, his hands finding a hold around Hugh's neck. He met those clear blue eyes levelly. "I will not risk you. I might be overthinking things—"

"We both like to plan ahead." Hugh shook his head, a soft smile drawing his mouth up. "I don't consider this overthinking. It's better if we can stay in contact. But this is something you can craft today?"

"The space of a few hours or so is all I need to make them. It's not a complex spell—well, I take that back, it's not simple either. But it's not horrendously complex like wards. Two or three hours to forge them into the desired shape and apply the spell work is sufficient."

"Do you mind if I design the look of them?"

Adrien blinked at this, not expecting the request. He didn't see a problem with it and nodded. "That's fine. You have a design in mind?"

"Half designed already. Just give me paper, pencil, and a bit of time and I can sketch it out for you."

Adrien would have made them simple and practical, so if his lover had a way to put their own stamp on them, then he didn't mind. "Then let's set to it. We've too much to do and not enough time to do it in."

Hugh smacked a kiss against his mouth. "We're sharing a cabin on the way home. Just so I have more time with you that isn't interrupted." Adrien and Hugh both craved more time together, and three weeks on a boat together was the perfect remedy. Adrien had no intention of portaling them home.

"I have no objections to that. For now..." Adrien sighed. "I suppose it's best to get this insanity over with."

SIXTEEN

It took a full day to make all the arrangements. Ribeiro had pulled together some mercenaries for hire, ones he'd used before and could vouch for. They met right after breakfast the next morning, geared up and ready to go. Adrien gave each of them a portable shield to help with not only fighting the American sorcerers, but worst case, the Mapinguari.

They all waited in a conference room inside of Ribeiro's office, the men chatting with each other, sitting about and at ease. Adrien could tell how used to jumping into the fray they were—the idea that they'd be in combat in five minutes or so didn't bother them overmuch. No nerves to be found here.

Hugh and Ribeiro were conferring over something in the other room, leaving Adrien to make the last-minute preparations. Adrien created the shield for the last man and turned to go back to the front of the room, only to find Cynric right at his elbow.

"I am not about to make you a shield," Adrien said, assuring his friend, tone dry.

"Ha-ha-ha, you're so funny." Cynric's dark brown eyes sparkled with impish delight. It was never a look that boded well for Adrien. "I noticed something interesting this morning. Hugh's wearing a new platinum necklace—"

Shite. Why was Cynric so observant? Why?

"—while my friend who doesn't wear jewelry at all is now sporting not only a ring of matching platinum, but a rather nicely tooled leather cuff with mithril. Fascinating change of behavior."

"Oh, do stop," Adrien said with a sigh.

"I really can't. I've never seen you like this before with anyone. It's the best entertainment I've had all week. You two are adorable in your honeymoon phase." Cynric threw an arm around Adrien's neck and hugged him in closer. Only in his ear did he say, "I really am happy that he reached you. He wasn't sure how to at first.

You'll have to tell me how later, when this is over and we have time to get drunk and talk."

Was it wrong of Adrien that he wanted to brag? He bit down on a smile. "After this."

"Good."

Hugh came back in with Ribeiro. It was Ribeiro who addressed the room—in Portuguese, so Adrien caught one word in fifty. He was good with the Asian languages, not the romance ones.

Coming to his side, Hugh leaned in and murmured, "He's explaining the gist of what to do. Are you ready?"

"I am."

Hugh looked to Cynric and got a confirming nod there as well. "Then open a portal, *mo ghràidh*. It's about time to wrap this up."

Mo ghràidh? Gaelic for "my love" if he wasn't mistaken. Adrien liked the endearment very much. He had to resist several impulses that would get them into trouble. Fortunately, he had a ready distraction at hand. Turning to the door, he weaved the portal spell, connecting it to the door of one of the village huts. He half expected it to go awry, to not connect at all. In the Americans' shoes, he would have reworked the ward to prevent this very thing. However, it connected seamlessly.

Were they dependent on deliveries coming through via portal? Was that why they hadn't changed anything? Either way, it shortened this task from three days to one minute, taking out the requirement of travel by river, so Adrien wasn't about to complain. Seemed the Americans were about as smart as the Chechen Brotherhood. Not dumb, per say, but stubborn and greedy to the point of stupidity. Perhaps all criminals were all of that mindset.

He nodded to Cynric, who would lead this charge. "Ready."

Cynric had his two trusted Tulwar swords in hand, a feral grin on his lips, and a rifle strapped to his back. The swords were not just metal, of course; no sorcerer specializing in combat would carry anything so mundane into battle. The swords had an eerie aura about them, like smoke rising from the metal, the smoke tinged a deep red. It gave the impression the swords were molten in the middle, radiating heat. Adrien knew from experience that one touch of those swords would cleave anything neatly in half—including a steel pole.

With something of a cackle, Cynric went straight through. Adrien and Hugh were quick on his heels, Hugh's revolver out and at the ready, a spell formed in Adrien's hand. Considering the density of the humidity in the Amazon Rainforest, he had just the spell to use here. His magic drew on all the water in the air and formed it into deadly icicles in his hand.

Of course the Americans weren't expecting a fight, so Adrien was able to get almost everyone through the portal before a shout of alarm went up. Adrien kept his shield up with one hand, icicle in the other, ready for a target to present itself. An American in a black cowboy hat obliged, running around the back end of a hut and coming into view. Adrien promptly put an icicle through his chest.

"They've gots a goddamned sorcerer!" someone yelled.

"Well, now, that's uncalled for," Adrien murmured, a wicked smile taking over his face.

Hugh fell back a few steps, putting himself solidly on Adrien's left, their shields overlapping. "I'll shoot the bastard who said that."

"Aww, Hugh, are you defending my honor?"

Hugh just winked at him, then lifted his gun and fired.

Men were taking cover now, or trying to, but there really wasn't anywhere to *take* cover. Going into a hut was idiotic as it became a kill box, staying outside the hut only meant you had thin wood boards as a barrier, and going outside the magical barrier was almost certain suicide as the Mapinguari would quickly be upon the fool. They hated noise, and with all this gunfire and screaming, they'd be sure to react. It was a lose-lose situation for the Americans.

Adrien didn't feel one iota of sympathy for them.

He stayed in step with Hugh as they worked their way down the main path. Two mercenaries were at their back, taking advantage of the overlapping shields and providing cover from behind. Adrien kept an eye on them, but they were competent fighters and doing rather well, so he didn't pay them much attention.

With all the mayhem announcing their arrival, the Americans seemed to explode inwards from every angle. Cynric was a whirling dervish, cutting down men before they could do much more than get a gun in their hands. Adrien fell in to cover his back, an old habit from their training days, aiming his icicles at people with clinical precision.

Hugh grunted before the report of his gun mixed in with the

other shots coming in. "More than I expected."

Yes, Adrien hadn't realized the Americans had this many people here either. He had only seen six when he'd been here with Hugh. Clearly, reinforcements had joined since then. A few Chinese workers were scattered about the place. Some of the men looked to be natives, no doubt here for a paycheck. Seemed a pity they'd pay with their lives instead.

Finally, a magical attack hit Adrien's shield. One of the sorcerers had made his entrance.

Turning, Adrien caught sight of a woman in cargo pants, her frizzy red hair up in a ponytail. She promptly threw another spell at him.

Whoops, his mistake—a sorceress had made *her* entrance. It didn't matter to Adrien the gender; anyone who picked a fight with him, he would oblige.

He blocked the first two spells, gauging her ability and finding it average. In fact, if Julian had been present, he would have likely won the fight with raw power alone. She was certainly no match for Adrien. He bounced off a third spell, amused at her obvious frustration.

"Ya damn prissy, fight like a man!" she snapped.

"Temper, temper," he murmured. "But if you insist."

Without compunction, he threw two high-powered spells at her, one after the other. First, one to disarm, which included knocking her rather mediocre shield out of the way. She'd put up only a front-facing shield, which was ludicrously stupid in this situation and easy for him to deal with. The second spell was a formed icicle he'd kept hovering over his hand. He shot it as straight as a bullet and with the same impact. It hit her solidly in the heart.

With a thump, she hit the ground, likely dead before impact.

All right, that was one sorcerer. Where was the other? A temporary barrier like this would require more than one to support it.

It was madness after that, with bullets flying in the air, the screams of the wounded and dying, the impact of bodies hitting wood or dirt only to lie absolutely still without even a breath to stir them. Adrien focused not on them, but on two things specifically: Cynric and Hugh.

Neither would fall on his watch.

Hot magic in the form of fire zinged toward Adrien's right side. He went to deflect it, moving on instinct, but his shield never felt the impact.

Cynric intercepted it smoothly, his swords cutting the arrow of fire cleanly in half, dissipating the spell before it could do anything more than wash over them in a wave of hot air. He threw his own spell in return, using one of his swords like a wand to throw an arc of blazing power back in the same direction. The sorcerer seemed to believe that hiding behind a rather large fern would be enough to snipe from, but it gave no protection, and in a second both bush and sorcerer were lit on fire. The man gave nothing more than a garbled scream before he, too, collapsed lifeless on the ground.

As suddenly as it all started, it stopped. Adrien went from fighting for his life one moment, only to turn and see not a single opponent to be had. He panned the area, carefully looking everywhere, but still no enemies. Were they done already?

Hugh's warm hand found his shoulder. "Are you well, *mo ghràidh*?"

"I am," Adrien said, looking him over as well. Hugh had sweat dotting his temples—inevitable in this humid heat—but other than that he barely looked mussed. "You?"

"I'm fine. That was almost anticlimactic." Hugh regarded the road they stood on, looking about. "Cynric, anything on your side?"

"Seems like we got them all. I mean, it makes sense not a lot of people would be here. They're clearly still in prep stages for mining." Cynric came back to them, arms lax at his sides. "I think we can leave it to our mercenaries to clear the rest of the camp, take on any stragglers we missed."

The Americans' sorcerers were definitely dead, since their ward was dissipating. It was as good as a death certificate, really. Adrien looked up, caught the ward before it could dissipate completely, and reinstated it. He and Cynric could carry it for a short while, until he could get his mithril over here to anchor it properly. Cynric could carry the ward by himself until Adrien returned, so long as he was quick. He had absolutely no interest in leaving the camp unprotected in the meantime.

Cynric swept an arm toward the tree line. "Adrien, let's go hunting for our furry ape friends."

Adrien wanted to do that about as much as he wanted to

dance upon an anthill, but needs must. He gave a short nod and headed for the exterior of the ward. It did not surprise him in the slightest that Hugh stayed right in step with him.

While they moved, Cynric sheathed both swords and changed to the rifle slung over his back. He fell into step on Hugh's other side.

"Hugh, you're a decent enough shot, you take them on if they get too close for me to use the rifle. I hope to snipe them from afar, but they're damn fast, as you've seen. Hard to get a bead on."

"I'll take any shot I can," Hugh assured him.

"Remember to make it a head shot." Cynric waved to the rest of his person. "Anywhere else, the bullet almost bounces off. Their hide is something else."

"Understood."

"Also remember to stay right next to me," Adrien said. He wanted the strength of his shields covering Hugh at all times.

Hugh deadpanned, "Yes, such a hardship."

Adrien poked him in the ribs. How dare the man tease him. Hugh just chuckled, enjoying himself.

They cleared the village ward with wariness, as they really couldn't predict where the Mapinguari might be. Adrien hoped they were close, just so he didn't have to chase them down in the thick foliage. Never pleasant, bearding the dragon in its own den.

"Walk along the route to the river?" Hugh suggested. "It's where we encountered it last time."

"Might as well," Adrien said. They had no better plan. He pulled a gun from his hip holster, also ready to fire. Despite his own meager skills with a gun, he'd learned through painful experience that for this, magic wasn't the best option.

"If you saw it here last, then it suggests they're staying close, trying to kill the intruders." Cynric had his rifle at the ready, eyes probing the thickness of the trees and underbrush ahead of them. "I don't really want to go into the jungle if we can help it— fuck!"

Adrien's head snapped in the direction his friend looked, and even then, he wasn't quite fast enough to get his gun up in time. The Mapinguari hit his ward hard, snarling and spinning off again, diving back into the shrubs beyond the tree line. The smell slammed into Adrien's nose even through the preventive layer on his shields and he gagged. Did expectant women feel like this? He had utter sympathy for them if that was the case.

It took effort to swallow the bile rising in his throat, to stay focused. He wanted this over with. He was not losing control over his shields and risking his friend or lover, either.

Cynric had his gun up, ready to fire at a moment's notice, the barrel slowly turning as he did. "I think I hear it. I just can't get eyes on it."

Hugh had his gun up as well. "Cynric, what if we bait and switch? I'll fire into the shrub, see if I can bait it out."

"I'm game to try."

Hugh fired twice in quick succession and to immediate results. The Mapinguari came at them with a roar, a full-frontal charge. Adrien fired at the same time Cynric did, the report of their shots overlapping. The Mapinguari reeled backward as it fell, dead before it hit the ground, toppling a sapling in its wake.

"Who actually got it?" Cynric asked. "You or me?"

"You're welcome to do an autopsy to determine it." Adrien frankly didn't care as long as it was dead and stayed dead.

Cynric gagged. "How dare you suggest that. I want to keep my breakfast in my stomach, thank you."

"You were the one wondering."

Cynric had his mouth open on some retort he promptly abandoned as he lifted his rifle and fired again.

Adrien looked frantically about, trying to find where his friend had aimed, mentally cursing a Mapinguari's speed. Hugh's gun barked a report, and not a second later there was a crash in the underbrush along with a deep, guttural groan that sounded like a death rattle.

"By Jove, Hugh, I think you got it." Cynric lowered his rifle a little before lifting it again, looking through the scope. "I can barely see its fur, and it doesn't look like it's breathing. I say we cautiously make an approach to verify."

"We have to," Adrien said. He didn't want to, but he couldn't work or rest easy in this place until he knew for sure that there was no Mapinguari ready to ambush him.

They slowly made their way off the trail, converging on the spot. The stench grew worse with every step until Adrien had to pinch his nose shut and breathe through his mouth just to keep from vomiting.

Cynric lifted up on tiptoes to see over a shrub and then sank back down. "Dead. Hugh got it right between the eyes. Let's get out of here."

Adrien was all too happy to leave the area, but he knew that they couldn't just leave the bodies to rot here. The smell alone would deter the workers. "Cyn, we need to burn them."

His friend was not amused. He was definitely pouting. "Must we?"

"We can set up a ward around the bodies so the fire doesn't spread, but yes, we must. Think of how this will smell three days from now, even. The poor workers coming onto this jobsite don't deserve to be assaulted in such a way."

"Fine, fine. You get the other one, I'll handle this one."

Adrien retreated to the first Mapinguari, quickly erecting a ward around its sprawled body—which helped with the smell alone—and gave it a once-over. Seemed quite dead, as blood was draining out of the second mouth on its stomach. The thing was even more grotesque than he remembered from his youth. The shaggy fur clumped together, bugs and such crawling all about its body. It even looked like parts of the fur were molding, as green and white fuzzies clung to the strands. This one was larger than usual for its species, well over seven feet tall, the monkey-ish face slack in death. As long as it was dead and wouldn't try to fight him off again, Adrien was satisfied. He lit the interior of the ward with a fire spell at its max setting. He wanted the body to burn to ash quickly.

There, that should do. Now all Adrien had to do was erect wards from the river to the campsite and then beyond to where the mines would be. It was so simply said, it didn't accurately reflect how much work that would entail. Cynric's help was the only thing that kept this from being a week-long project. Hmm, perhaps he should call Julian back. It would be good practice and a consolation for being sent away after being promised an adventure.

"We might as well start at the river and then work our way to the village as I set up the wards." Adrien gestured in the direction of the river in question, just out of sight of where they stood. "I've got a mithril ingot on me, so I can establish something temporarily until we have the time to make a more permanent ward."

"Will you need both hands to make the ward?"

That was a strange question out of his lover's mouth. "Uh, no?"

"Capital." Hugh promptly reached down and took Adrien's

hand in his, threading their fingers together.

Adrien looked down at their joined hands, his own fingers reflexively closing about that warm, calloused hand. He'd never in his life held hands with a man like this.

He liked it immensely.

Smiling up at Hugh, he said without reproach, "You are utterly incorrigible."

"You bring out the best in me, what can I say?" Hugh grinned back.

Adrien snorted. Seriously, this man. He tugged them into motion, as they really had to get wards up, and he wanted out of the rainforest sooner rather than later. Eventually, he'd need to let go of Hugh's hand. But before that time came, he'd enjoy every moment.

SEVENTEEN

Julian was utterly delighted to be back in the Amazon Rainforest and working. Mac had come too, of course, and promptly went off with Sir Hugh to do engineering things. Julian finally got to do some higher magic on this trip.

The village was much, much smaller than he'd anticipated. Perhaps a dozen huts altogether, and they were for the most part single-room structures. They looked old, rickety, and one good storm away from toppling over. Was he still excited about being here? Absolutely.

Exploring a rainforest had been something outside of his wildest dreams. The air was thick with humidity, the scent of green growing things, and birdsong. It felt rather like he'd entered another dimension. It sparked his adventuresome spirit and fanned a flame. After this, he was absolutely going to explore the world as much as he could.

"First, we'll lay the foundation for the new ward," Adrien said. He waved a dismissive hand at the one overhead. "This one is insufficient."

Julian craned his head back to look above them. The ward was a light, shimmering dome that covered the area. It seemed to be working just fine? "What's wrong with it?"

"Two things. First, it's not large enough. It only covers this area, and we need it to extend to not only the mine, but the river."

Ah. All right, he could see why this needed to be replaced, then. "What's the second issue?"

"It doesn't have the right security on it." Adrien put a hand to Julian's shoulder and shifted to stand at his side. He pointed directly ahead at a patch near the path. "You see the inscriptions there?"

He did. They were written in lines of glowing magic. Julian was still learning all the symbols and characters, but he could recognize about half. "I do. It says...predators out?"

"Very good. Can you read anything else of it?"

"Um...something about all portal spells allowed?"

"Also correct. We want to nix the second one now. I was able to bring in a full posse of people and attack because of that clause. If we left it like that, anyone else would be able to do the same, and I don't want these workers open to attack after we leave."

It was a very wise precaution. "Will we outlaw portaling altogether?"

"Hmm, no, that's not the best option. In case of emergency, they'll need to go back and forth." Adrien let his hand drop and pointed to the nearest hut. "That will be the front office, or so I'm told. I'll anchor a portal spell there so they can go to a single point in Macapá. With an anchored spell like that, I can instruct the ward to make that point as an exception. That way if there's an injury, or they need supplies, they can come and go."

Smart. Then again, his master was a very smart man. Julian hoped and dreamed to be like him one day.

"All right, I've set the ward points along the river walk, so that's ready to go. I'll teach you how to create a ward's anchor. It's by far the easiest part of the spell. If you can master that then we'll be able to get this done much faster."

Julian gave him a determined nod. "I'm ready. What do I do?"

"First, craft it like so..."

The spike was pure energy, nothing more than a signature of power. Adrien drove it sharply into the soft ground with a single flick of his hand. It did indeed look simple, rather similar to some of Julian's magic exercises. He lifted his platinum wand, formed a spike, held it, let Adrien modify it. Dropped it, tried again, and got it right on the second try. Then he walked to where Adrien pointed before dropping the spike into the ground.

"Good!" Adrien applauded. "Again. We'll keep walking and doing this. I'll take over when you tire. It's best to take turns and spell each other when creating a massive ward like this."

"All right."

The first half hour, they didn't say much. Julian appreciated it as he was trying very hard to focus. After they switched, however, Adrien now driving the spikes in, he felt it safe enough to talk. It wasn't like Adrien needed to concentrate on the task as much as Julian did.

"Master, can I ask?"

"You can always ask." Adrien's brow quirked in amusement.

Right, he should know that by now. Adrien never told him to hold his tongue. "Are you happy?"

"Very much so. Ah, you mean because of Hugh?"

It was nice to see him smile like that, as if he had no fears. Julian felt a little butterfly in his stomach because of it. "Yes."

Adrien drove a spike into the ground and then paused, expression pensive. "I am very bad with interpersonal relations, as you know. I think as much joy as it brings me to have such a good man in my life, it's also a relief. Hugh has seen me at my best, and my worst, and still only holds the highest opinion of me. I never thought I would have a lover such as him. I'm not even sure what I did to deserve him."

His master, seriously. Why did he not understand? Adrien might be abrasive at moments, that was true, but he was also incredibly affectionate and loyal. And Julian hoped he himself might find a lover in the future who was like his master.

"I do know"—Adrien continued walking to the next spot—"that I won't give anyone else the opening to take him from me. There will, in fact, be hell to pay if someone tries."

"That's the spirit, Master." Julian approved of this wholeheartedly. "Will you tell people aside from us?"

"I will. What members of my family whom I'm close to, a few select friends. Hugh will do the same. We won't advertise it to the world, but we won't keep it secret from our inner circle, either. That's our stance."

"I see. I'm glad."

Adrien drove a spike in and paused, looking at him through narrowed eyes. "I hope that when you and MacMallin find someone for yourselves, you'll do the same."

"Ehhh? Why do you think I'll be able to find someone?" Former prostitute and street rat that he was, Julian didn't give it good odds.

Adrien rolled his eyes as if Julian had just said something nonsensical. "First of all, you are now a Danvers. That alone will garner you attention in society."

Oh. Well, that was likely true.

"Secondly, you will become a far more powerful sorcerer than I—"

Julian had heard him say this before but had always assumed it was Adrien's way of building his confidence or something. But in that moment, his master seemed perfectly sincere. "Ehhhh?!"

"—and you are in good standing with Prince Henry besides, and why are you reacting like that? I've told you before that you have more raw power than I do."

"No, but, but," he spluttered, the shock making him dumb in thought. "Master! Surely not by that much. I thought you were being kind."

Adrien regarded him as if he'd just said something stupid again. "Julian. I felt you eight streets away, *untrained*, without you even trying to use a spell. That's how powerful you are. Six, eight years from now, and you will be my direct competition in business. I promise you this."

He'd thought Adrien had been exaggerating matters when he'd spoken on this before. Maybe bragging about his apprentice a little. He hadn't thought Adrien meant every word of it. "Oh. Um. Is that all right?"

"Of course. There's always someone better. I never set out to be the best sorcerer in the world, you know."

"As competitive as you are, you expect me to believe that?"

"I truly don't want to be the best in the world," Adrien said, pausing to remove a shrub with a spell before putting another spike down. "Too much work. And people ask you to do dangerous, insane things."

Ah, well, that was likely true.

"I just have to be better than most of my business rivals," Adrien said. "Because like hell will I let them look down on me or think they can take business from me."

See? Very competitive. Julian likely didn't fall into the bracket of rival because he was an apprentice and thereby one of Adrien's people. Fortunately, in many senses, as he'd hate to be on the wrong side of this man.

The ring on Adrien's hand sparkled with a dim light.

"*Adrien?*"

Adrien lifted the ring up to his mouth. "Yes, dearest?"

The way he answered made Julian's heart flutter again. It was so sweet to see his master openly in love.

"*Are you nearing the mine's entrance?*"

"We are, in fact, perhaps a stone's throw away. Why? Is there a particular thing you want me to do there?"

"*There is, and it's rather hard to explain. I'll bring Mac along and catch up in a moment.*"

"Meet you at the cave's entrance, then." Adrien let the connection drop. He glanced at Julian and sighed, head lolling back on his shoulders as if praying to any god listening. "Oh, do stop looking at me like that."

"Like what?" Julian asked like he didn't know.

"Like *that*. You and Anastasia act as giddy as if you were the ones in the relationship."

"We just like seeing you happy." Julian had no defense for it. After spending months fearing Adrien would never open his heart up to a man, watching him with Sir Hugh was both a relief and a joy. Julian might have also won the bet, as Mac had thought it would take another six months for Hugh to wear Adrien down. Julian very much looked forward to a whole week of not doing dishes.

"You're acting like I've found a unicorn, or the Holy Grail, or some other such thing. The smugness radiating from you is absurd."

Well, Julian had worked hard behind the scenes nudging both Adrien and Hugh in the right direction. He deserved to be smug, didn't he?

Adrien muttered and kept working as they moved forward. Julian followed along, spelling him briefly at one point, and tried not to look so smug. He had a feeling he was rather bad at it. Just from the sideways looks Adrien kept giving him.

They met up with Sir Hugh and Mac at the mouth of the mine's entrance, which really looked like a man-made cave, the edges of it jagged and bare of all overgrowth—a rare sight in this rainforest. The opening didn't look all that large, though, barely wide enough for two men abreast, and perhaps five feet tall. Surely this wasn't the main entrance?

"Adrien." Hugh smiled like he hadn't just seen the man two hours ago. "How goes it?"

"Quite on schedule. Julian's speeding the process along. What was your thought?"

"I wish to protect the workers in case of a cave collapse. Is there anything you can offer to help safeguard them? Or give them a way out if something does go wrong?"

"Hmm, yes, I can think of a few things."

Julian tried to pay attention as his master rattled off possibilities, but his attention kept being diverted downward. Even while they talked business, Hugh and Adrien casually held hands. It was entirely unconscious on their parts, like they couldn't resist the urge to touch when given the chance.

It was, in a word, adorable.

Mac sidled in closer to Julian and whispered, "I didn't know grown men could be cute, but they're proving me wrong."

"Agreed," Julian whispered back. "And to think Master was fighting us on this for months."

"Thank god Master Hugh was able to get past all his walls." Mac draped an arm over Julian's shoulder, getting comfortable.

Julian leaned into the contact. He liked it when Mac did this, as he liked the skinship very much. Mac had always been his protector, ever since they'd met, and he felt more secure with him than anyone else in the world. Even if such contact proved a tad too hot in this humid air, Julian wasn't the least bit tempted to move.

Sir Hugh turned to them, a copper brow quirked in challenge. "And what did we just say needed to be done, boys?"

Without missing a beat, Mac rattled off, "Emergency portation spells strewn throughout the mine, alarm beacon at the mine's entrance, building with safety and rescue gear to be stored near the alarm."

Thank god he'd been paying attention because Julian had missed most of that. "What he said."

Adrien's expression suggested he knew full well Julian hadn't really been paying attention, but he let it slide. "Hugh, mark where you want to build things. Julian and I will start with the portation spells inside. Come along, Julian, back to work."

He happily did as bid, following his master inside. Did this count as spelunking? He was going inside a cave, after all.

Hopefully there weren't any bats inside. Flying creatures overhead were a no in his book.

Well, if there were, he was sure that Adrien could deal with them. All Julian had to do was make sure to not get lost. If he did, Mac would never let him live it down.

EIGHTEEN

Hugh stepped out of the minuscule bathroom attached to their cabin and paused in the doorway, a towel around his neck. He'd booked the two of them a larger cabin for the trip home and was thankful for it, as they'd put the queen-sized bed to good use. The sight of Adrien in their bed, sleeping so peacefully, arrested him in place. He'd dreamed often of this very moment the past few months, of seeing his lover in peaceful repose, but this was so much better than his dreams. Knowing he didn't have to wake up to find a different reality, that he could instead cross the five steps to the bed and rejoin Adrien, was so much sweeter.

They were still finding their footing with each other, but they'd been a couple barely a week so that was to be expected. With the Mapinguari dead, Americans dealt with, and the wards up, there was nothing left for them to do. Hugh's cautious estimation of a month of work proved to be a vast overestimation. No one complained about the work being done early because they were all ready to go home. They'd boarded the ship yesterday, and Hugh and Adrien had spent the majority of their time aboard in this very cabin, only venturing out for meals. He hadn't even had to ban the boys from bothering them, as both had given him a cheeky wink and kept to their own devices.

Having Adrien's attention without distraction felt like a gift to Hugh. When his lover wasn't wrangling teenage boys or didn't have a case hanging over his head, he was very fun company. Hugh was smug that Adrien's guard had dropped significantly around him. He'd thought the man relaxed around him before he confessed—turned out it wasn't even comparable to the Adrien of now.

What would it be like six months from now? A year? Ten years? When they were utterly comfortable with each other, knew the other well. The idea brought a smile to Hugh's face. He relished the thought.

Adrien cracked open one eye before closing it again, still snug in the bed and not apparently interested in moving. "What are you smiling at?"

"You."

"Ridiculous."

Adrien said that, but a smile curved his lips up in a pleased way.

Hugh tossed his towel back into the bathroom's hamper before returning to the bed, sliding naked in between the sheets. Adrien accommodated him, shifting about on his side until he was tucked in against Hugh's chest. Lifting a hand, Hugh carded silky black hair from Adrien's forehead, indulging in his ability to touch as he liked.

"When we return to England, I want to host a dinner party," Hugh declared without segue. "So that all my family and friends might meet you."

Those dark brown eyes looked back at him steadily. "You say 'meet' and yet for some reason I hear 'show off.'"

That's because Adrien had quite acute hearing. "I can't?"

"You are so incorrigible." Snorting a laugh, Adrien lifted enough to kiss Hugh's shoulder.

He'd take that as a yes. Hugh had learned over time that unless Adrien said a direct no, then it was a yes. He'd gotten quite good at translating him.

"I'll invite family and friends over as well so they might meet you. If luck is with me, I'll have time to do that and anchor our portals before a case descends upon me."

Hugh knew Adrien often had no warning before a case dropped in his lap, so he acknowledged this with a nod. "Speaking of, which of my residences will you connect to?"

"Which one are you at the most?"

"Isle of Man, really. Like you, I barely use my London flat unless business takes me there. If I am in London, I tend to stay with my mother."

"Hmm. Well, any doorway—with the right knob design—can support up to five portals. I can in theory connect them all, but I'd like to connect at least one to my Thai home. If I'm going to be in England for long stretches of time, portaling home every now and again to check on the house and enjoy warm air would be delightful."

"It means traveling there by conventional means before you can anchor the portal, though, doesn't it?"

"Eh, no, not necessarily. I can in theory do it remotely, it's just an insane power drain. I'll have to offset the drain with a large quantity of mithril. Which I fortunately have, thanks to my generous lover." Adrien's eyes twinkled in unspoken laughter. "In any case, it's doable, I just need to spend a full two days setting it all up."

"You really must explain the mechanics of how this works. Why is the doorknob design important?"

"Hugh, is there anything in this world you don't want to understand? Any function you just accept as long as it works?"

Adrien was half teasing, but Hugh said honestly, "Not a blessed thing."

"Always the engineer."

"If it makes me money, I'll do it all."

Snorting a laugh, Adrien acquiesced. "I'll try to explain, but stop me when I no longer make sense."

It might seem like strange pillow talk to anyone else, but to Hugh, this was how he and Adrien thought. This was how they planned for the future, how they guaranteed that they could always be connected to each other. To him, every word out of his lover's mouth was music to his heart.

Hugh settled in, Adrien a warm weight in his arms, and savored every note.

Nineteen

Twenty days aboard the ship to London, able to indulge in Hugh, left Adrien only aching for more. More time, more chances to bask in this man's affections. Adrien had been half afraid that twenty days in his company would make Hugh tire of him, or perhaps regret their relationship, but it had only made their bond stronger. He felt far more secure with Hugh than he'd ever felt with a lover. It wasn't even a competition. His only regret upon leaving the boat was that he now had to share Hugh with other people.

It was not, by any means, a reality he liked the taste of. Which could be why he headed home with a firm plan in mind.

Adrien only deviated once, and that was to portal to Emily and George's country estate to fetch Darby. His boys were dying to have their dog back, Darby was ecstatic to see her people again, and George's children were crying and begging to keep her. Adrien should have expected the last one. Darby was a very sweet dog, so of course the young tykes would get attached. Which meant an immediate headache for George and Emily. Before the situation became more of a fiasco, Adrien gave apologies and quickly portaled all three of his people plus dog to his flat.

And so, they were finally home.

Now, anyone could tell you Adrien was a practical man by nature. He liked having things sorted, to have everything in place, and found it hard to relax until it was done. That being said, what did he do the day after they returned to England?

Started anchoring his door portal.

Hugh, having announced he had no intention of going to his own flat, leaned a shoulder against the foyer wall to watch as a kneeling Adrien took the front door's handle apart. Hugh seemed amused, for some reason, a small smile playing around his mouth.

"At it already?"

Adrien focused on the screwdriver in his hand and the screw he was taking out. He sniffed dismissively. "I refuse to let something as mundane as *logistics* keep us apart."

"I truly do adore you."

"Oh stop." Adrien refused to turn and reveal he was blushing. Hugh might go on about how Adrien never left him in doubt of his feelings, but the Scot was worse than him.

Julian arrived with a crate full of things, which he set on the floor with a clatter. "Master, all of this?"

Adrien glanced over to double-check. Mithril, air filaments, and clear crystals. "Very good, that's exactly what we need. Now, as soon as I have this knob off—"

It came away from the door and into his hand, the metal solid and heavy in his palm. Adrien grunted in satisfaction and rose to his feet. "Splendid. Julian, measure the circumference and depth of the knob itself. Then calculate how to split the knob evenly into four sections."

Julian looked game until that last direction, then paused uncertainly. It was understandable, of course; the lad had just learned division. Adrien had learned that practical math problems, in real world work, often made the lessons stick better. Besides, it was good practice in magic, too.

"Why four?" Julian asked in confusion.

Ah, that was the sticking point. "For the four places we wish to go. Hugh's house, my home in Bangkok, and Anastasia's."

"Oh. Wait, that's three."

"We have to anchor the spell to here. Hence, four."

Understanding dawned. "Now that makes sense. All right, I'll measure it."

"Once you are finished, hand it to Hugh."

"Am I working on this too?" Hugh didn't seem to mind in the least.

Adrien gave him a droll look. "My lover is a mechanical genius. Of course I'll make use of you."

Hugh chuckled, highly entertained by this. "And what am I doing to it?"

"I need you to do two things. First, a spring installed inside, something we can activate by pushing the knob in to switch settings. Second, a solid division between the four spaces that can be chosen."

"Hmm, yes, that's easy enough. I'll draw Mac into the project. Where is he, anyway?"

"Walking Darby," Julian said. "He should be back soon."

"I'll set up in the workroom, then, while waiting." Hugh took all the pieces of the doorknob with him, carting them to the very back room of the flat.

Some people might worry about leaving a door unguarded when there was no proper way to close or lock it, but Adrien did not. For one, he lived in a very protected building, with a guard at the door, so there shouldn't be any ruffians roaming about the halls. Also, everyone in the building knew who he was, and only the foolish would dare test his temper.

Besides, once Darby returned, she would alert him to anyone at the door. She was enthusiastic about announcing anyone who approached their flat.

Right, then, time to craft the magical inner workings while Hugh did the mechanical bits—

There came a tentative knock on the front door. "Uh, excuse me? Anyone home?"

Adrien wasn't expecting callers. He opened the door, curious who might be on the other side, to find a courier in a sharp white-and-black uniform. The gangly boy seemed the same age as Julian and MacMallin and appeared uncertain as he stood in the hall.

"Adrien Danvers' residence?" the boy asked, eyes constantly darting to the open space where a doorknob should be.

"You're at the right place." Adrien indicated the gaping hole. "Just some renovations. I'm Adrien Danvers."

His confusion cleared. "Ah, right then. If you'll sign here, sir."

Adrien accepted the clipboard, signed to confirm delivery, then took the very heavy and embossed envelope before closing the door. How strange. Only the very upper crust used such paper, but he hadn't many acquaintances from—oh. That crest pressed into the wax was of the Danverses. And he doubted George would go through such trouble.

"Fucking hell," Adrien muttered, unceremoniously ripping the envelope open.

Julian leaned over his arm to see. "Isn't that the Danvers crest?"

"Indeed. I'll bet you anything it's from my father—" He unfolded the paper and sighed, resigned. "I for once wanted to be wrong."

"What does it say?"

A great deal Julian shouldn't hear, as it was mostly derogatory terms. Even Adrien inwardly winced at a few phrases, and he expected such from the overbearing man who'd sired him. Adrien paraphrased. "He says he's very unhappy with you and MacMallin being adopted in as Danverses and I am to attend him at his residence at once."

Julian looked at him uncertainly. "Will you go?"

"The man can sit there and rot for all I care. In fact, I hope he does. He's a blight upon humanity and the sooner we can put him into a grave, the better for all of us." Adrien lit the paper on fire with a simple spell and tossed it into the rubbish bin, letting it burn out. "He lost all control over me when he threw me out of the house. I will not give that control back to him."

Dusting his hands of the matter, he put on a smile. "Now. Let's go back to working a portal spell. Much more important."

Julian didn't look as reassured as he'd hoped. "But what if he gets mad you didn't go?"

"Then he's mad. I assure you, Julian, there's nothing that man can do to me. Now come, we have to carve the crystals first and they must be precisely the right size, otherwise they won't fit. If all four of us work on this steadily, we could have it done within two days, and then I can finally take you to my home in Bangkok."

Julian's attention was immediately diverted. "Just like that?"

"Certainly, the portal spell will be anchored. Nothing stopping us at that point. Don't you want to lounge on a beach, eat interesting new foods, and do nothing responsible for a few days?"

"Well, Master, if you put it like *that*..."

Hugh was possibly more dedicated than the boys in crafting the portal knob. Really, it was a matter of debate, but he felt equally keen to visit Thailand. He wanted to see what Adrien's true home looked like. He wanted to be somewhere else where the prying eyes and ears of other people didn't matter. Spending two more days indulging in Adrien's company felt like a gift before they all had to go back to work.

That said, the very moment the doorknob was put back into place at Adrien's flat, Hugh had a packed suitcase sitting nearby. He had no doubt the portal would work. He'd never seen Adrien fail with magic, and he knew for a fact his lover had tested each part of it to make sure it worked as designed, even as he put the pieces back together.

Adrien pushed the knob in, turned to the bright gold quadrant labeled *Thailand*, and then swung the door open.

What lay beyond was a scene Hugh had only heard descriptions of, and words had failed to do it any kind of justice.

Adrien had warned it was the start of monsoon season in Thailand, but they were lucky today, as it was clear skies. Barely a cloud in the sky, in fact.

The door opened into a garden, with luscious plants and trees lining a thick wall. It looked very established, as if the garden had been there a hundred years or more. Peeking out from behind the colorful flowers stretched a long, slatted walkway leading directly to a large wooden house. It seemed lifted up on stilts above the water surrounding it. The center part of the house was the largest, with smaller rooms branching out to either side that were slightly higher with each iteration. The roof was very steep, the edges of it sharp and pointed.

"That's your house?" MacMallin spluttered, eyes in danger of falling out of their sockets altogether. "It's huge!"

"It's not small," Adrien said, stepping through. "Now, boys, mind me when I say you're not allowed into a boat until I've drown-proofed you. Travel by boat is common here, more common than hailing a taxi in England, but I don't want you in danger of drowning if it overturns."

A danger Hugh hadn't thought of, but considering the house was surrounded by water on at least three sides...a good precaution to take.

Hugh took his suitcase in hand and followed Adrien out, closing the door behind him. Only then did he turn and realize the door on this side was a gate. Front gate leading in from the road? He could see evidence of a road through the metal slats.

He stretched out his legs to catch up with Adrien. "You didn't connect directly to the house?"

"Can't," Adrien said, leading him onto the wooden bridge. "The doors of the house are very, very traditional and don't have knobs in the English sense of the word. Just latches."

"Ahhh. That would make it difficult to connect."

"I can do so in a pinch, of course, but for a permanent portal, the garden gate was the better choice. Besides, my housekeeper—P'Bau, lovely woman—she threatened me with a tanning if I scared her again by popping through a door without warning."

MacMallin snickered behind them. "How many times have you scared her, Master?"

"Too many times, apparently." Adrien shrugged, not at all bothered by this. "Anyway, come in. I'll give you the grand tour."

Hugh was all too curious about how the house would look on the inside, so he kept right in step with him. Darby bounded ahead, pausing to sniff every two steps, tail wagging in excitement. Good thing they had a walled-in garden. The collie was bound to get distracted and lost otherwise.

Exiting the bridge, Hugh saw a rather lovely courtyard, with a low seating table circled by pillows and a small portico acting as shade. Beyond that, the main doors of the house stood wide open. There was a lip at the bottom, the doors made so that they folded in, pushed to either side. No one seemed to be home as Adrien entered, even though he called out a greeting in Thai. Perhaps shopping? Adrien had explained he kept a housekeeper and gardener in residence while he was away.

Hugh turned his head as he took it all in. The home was predominantly wood, sanded smooth and polished, with very tall ceilings. Even the furniture was wood, with brightly colored cushions in reds and greens stacked on it. It was cooler inside, and Hugh recognized the anti-mosquito and cooling charms painted on the very far wall. Of course Adrien would put them up in this tropical country.

Adrien waved to places as they passed through. "Kitchen, bathroom, and the rooms winging off to each side are bedrooms. Pick which one you like, boys, it makes no difference to me."

"We will," MacMallin said. "I think I want the one on the far end. Come on, Darby!"

Boys and dog moved off to explore.

Most of the house was very traditional, but Adrien had updated the kitchen and bathroom to be modern in function. And why not? Comfort and utility came first and foremost. Hugh certainly appreciated it. He despised outhouses as a matter of principle.

"As for you..." Adrien gave him an arch look. "You come with me."

"Well, I'd hope so." Hugh grinned back. "If you put me in another room, I'd assume I'd done something very wrong."

"As you should. But you've been quite good, so you stay with me. And I don't know why you packed. I'm putting you in traditional Thai clothes."

He was? "Why?"

"The second you spend any time outdoors, you'll thank me. European clothes are meant to hold heat in, and trust me, that's the last thing you want in Thailand."

Ah. Likely true. Well, he was quite all right with Adrien dressing him. And undressing him.

Adrien's bedroom looked lavish. No other word for it. The bed had a large canopy, likely a mosquito net, surrounding it. There was a thin looking mattress, the bedding made of...silk? It also boasted a stunning and vibrant swirling pattern. There were chests and a dresser, all of them with elaborate inlays of birds and flowers in the darkly polished wood. The room looked rather like a prince's abode.

No wonder Adrien preferred Thailand.

"Now, I called ahead and gave P'Bau your measurements, and she said she'd—ah-ha, there they are." Adrien went straight to one of the chests, which had two bundles sitting on top of it, and pulled one of the bundles up. It was dark blue in color, with a diamond sort of pattern in off-white, very intricate and masculine. It looked... "Isn't that a tad short?"

"You don't wear full pants here," Adrien explained. "It's supposed to hit the knees."

"But the shirt has full sleeves?"

"To protect against the sun and flies, yes."

"Ahhh. Well, it looks quite striking. How do I put it on?"

"First..." Adrien came in closer, hooking fingers in Hugh's belt and tugging him in with a wicked smile. "You must take this off."

His lover was entirely too pleased to have him here. Note that Hugh was not at all complaining. "Well, I'm sure you'll help with that. Won't you?"

"It'll be my *pleasure*," Adrien purred.

Hopefully the boys didn't choose to interrupt anytime soon. Hugh had a feeling trying on his new outfit was going to take a while.

The housekeeper, P'Bau, arrived, and she had been out buying groceries. She'd been expecting them, hence coming in with all sorts of things for them to eat. She struck Hugh as a motherly sort of person, and it wasn't just because of her older countenance. She wore no-nonsense clothes, hair up in a simple bun, and moved about the house while keeping track of them with a very practiced air. Adrien introduced everyone, and she immediately offered the boys food, which was happily accepted. Really, she had the boys wrapped around her finger in two seconds flat.

Adrien was snagged by the gardener (P'Bau's husband, apparently) as there was something about the house that needed fixing. Hugh didn't understand a single word in Thai—it was tone and expression that told him something was awry. He let Adrien attend to whatever it was, settling at the table in the courtyard. It was a perfectly beautiful day, and it seemed a waste to sit inside.

He had a cheat sheet of Thai words, written by Adrien, so he worked on memorizing them. Hugh absolutely detested walking about in a foreign country and not knowing any of the language. Besides, he wanted to learn it anyway, just to put a smile on Adrien's face.

P'Bau—he understood the Phi was meant as an honorific for anyone older—came to him and set down a cup of cool tea, along with something that looked very pretty. It was white, small, and round in shape, and supposedly edible?

P'Bau spoke in her heavily accented English, enunciating carefully. "This is khanom khrok."

Still no idea what that was, but it had never stopped Hugh before. He lifted one up and bit into it. The outside was crisp, but the inside was this light, creamy filling that tasted of sweet coconut. He hummed in approval, letting the flavor linger in his mouth. "It's delightful. *Kapunkhrab.*"

She grinned at him. "Good. You speak well."

"You are kind. I barely speak anything." He gestured to the sheet. "But I will learn."

Looking it over, she nodded in approval. "You are smart man.

Khun Adrien, he tell me about you, and children, before you come. I know he happy. I wish for long time he find man like you."

So apparently Adrien trusted his employees here enough to tell them about their relationship, which was good to know. "You flatter me, P'Bau."

"You kind man. That obvious." She beamed at him. "He smile at you. Love in his eyes. Very obvious."

Yes, well, she had him there.

Leaning in, she lowered her tone, casting a glance back at the house as if to make sure she wasn't going to be overheard. "Khun Adrien have friend here he sometimes beds. That man no good. You run him off when he comes."

Adrien had mentioned something about him, but it had been so casual and off the cuff, Hugh had barely paid it any mind. But if she was warning him... "I will. But why is he no good?"

"He treat Khun Adrien like property." P'Bau straightened with a disdainful snort. "I think Khun Adrien lonely. Why he put up with it."

Was there seriously even a single man in Adrien's life—aside from himself—who didn't ride roughshod over him? Hugh groaned. "I see. I will take care of him."

"Good. He always come quickly after Khun Adrien return—" Her head lifted, turning to face the gate. "*Shia*. There he come."

Hugh turned to sit sideways at the table, looking where she did. There was a man who had come through the main gate and was even now quickly crossing the bridge. He was clearly Thai with that tanned skin and black hair, and the closer he got, the better Hugh's view of him. He seemed to be roughly Hugh's age, pep in his step as if eager to come.

So this was the man who felt he had a claim on Adrien, eh? He was handsome, very much so. Even Hugh could see the arrogance in his face without P'Bau's warning.

She hissed at him, "Do not let him in. He snake."

P'Bau really, really didn't like this man. Hugh took her warning to heart. "Trust me, his involvement with Adrien ends today."

The second the man was off the bridge, he zeroed in on the housekeeper, ignoring Hugh entirely. "Bau," the man said loudly. He rattled something off in Thai, his tone almost condescending, like he spoke to an inferior being.

Now, this man had to be at least ten years younger than P'Bau, and he spoke to her so disrespectfully? No wonder she didn't like him. He was very rude.

She looked more and more upset as the man talked, saying something sharply in return, sounding like a denial. He in turn got frustrated, shifting so that he could push past her.

Hugh quickly stood, thrusting out an arm to stop him, and used what limited Thai he had. "*Bai mai.*"

The man stopped dead, head tilting back so he could look Hugh in the eye. "And who are you to bar my path?"

Oh, thank God, the man spoke impeccable English. That would make this easier. "My name is Hugh Quartermain. I understand you're here to see Adrien?"

The man looked him up and down and smirked, as if superior in his stance. "I assure you, I have a very *special* relationship with Adrien."

This fucking asshole. P'Bau was right, he was the kind of man who had human sacrifice written all over him. Hugh tapped the platinum necklace around his neck, with its obvious magical engraving, and gave the man an arch look in return. "I can assure *you*, your relationship has come to an end. Adrien Danvers is mine."

The man stared at the necklace, a vivid red heat of anger invading his face. "You're his lover?"

"I am."

"Ha! I bet you're only his lover in Europe. I am—"

Adrien's voice was hard and smooth, coming from the main door of the house. "You are not on the same level."

Hugh turned, watching as Adrien stalked toward them. Oh dear, his lover had a fiery light in his eyes that usually preceded violence and mayhem. Hopefully the house would still be intact after this argument.

The man faltered, staring at Adrien in confusion. "What do you mean by that?"

"You are not on his level," Adrien repeated slowly, as if explaining something to a rather slow-witted child. "I indulged you, as we both benefited from it, but our relationship has come to an end. Part of the reason I came back today was to tell you that."

The anger in the man rose to a higher level. "You can't possibly mean you've chosen him over me!"

"That's precisely what I mean." Adrien stopped dead in front of him, standing his ground, not the least bit intimidated. "Narong, I made it clear last time that I did not want to see you again. I thought you didn't believe me then. I came today to make sure you understood I meant it. You've disrespected my people too many times. I will not have you in my house again."

So this had been ongoing? This breakup? Well, Hugh felt better for that, but he could tell Narong didn't like it one bit.

Narong's temper visibly snapped, and he lunged for Adrien. Of course Adrien dodged backward, his reflexes keeping him out of reach. Hugh wasn't about to leave this fight completely up to Adrien. He didn't need Hugh's help, but he had it regardless.

Hugh lashed his hand out, finding and latching on to the man's throat before he lifted him up onto his toes. Narong thrashed, choking, trying to pry Hugh's hand off and failing utterly. He quite liked the man squirming like this—prey snared by his hand. He'd like it even better if he could just toss the lout in a deep hole somewhere and forget he ever existed.

In the coldest tone he'd ever used in his life, he snarled, "You either turn and walk away, never returning to this house, or I throw you in the river and you can swim back home. Which is it?"

Narong thrashed some more, expression a cross between anger and fear. He finally croaked, "Wa-walk."

"Good choice." Hugh let go, dropping him roughly onto his heels, and indicated the bridge with a jerk of his chin. "Go."

He was not a happy man, Narong. He glared at Hugh, tried one more silent, desperate plea with Adrien. But Adrien was entirely unmoved by those pleading eyes and just rolled his.

Without any toehold here, Narong finally surrendered. Shoulders slumped, he turned on his heel, eyes down as he trudged back across the bridge.

"*Ai'sut*," Adrien muttered under his breath. "I truly should not pick men up at bars after three drinks. My judgement is apparently awful at that point."

"You're not picking men up at bars ever again," Hugh corrected him. "I'm quite the jealous type."

Adrien brightened. "True, those days are long behind me. Thank Buddha."

Hugh, personally, was thrilled Adrien had stood up for himself. He hadn't known what to expect in this case, as Adrien seemed used to people treating him ill. But his lover had not given his former paramour the least bit of sympathy. Hugh wasn't sure what the cause was, per se, and he didn't flatter himself into thinking he was the main reason for Adrien's newfound strength. Still, he hoped he'd contributed to this new confidence.

Either way, Adrien had realized he deserved love and respect, and Hugh couldn't be more pleased if someone had offered him a million pounds.

Turning to his housekeeper, Adrien gave a bow. "P'Bau, I heard him saying awful things to you. I'm so sorry. I threw him out of the house last time because of that."

She waved him off. "He gone. I happy."

Hugh had the sense that if the young lout had come with an apology, and Hugh hadn't been there, Adrien might have forgiven Narong and continued their arrangement. Thank God Hugh and Adrien had gotten thrown together in a hole in the Amazon. At least that had prevented such a toxic relationship from continuing.

Adrien's hand found his and gave a squeeze, his expression apologetic. He needn't feel sorry; Hugh was quite pleased to take the trash out.

"Sit with me." Hugh drew Adrien to the table. "You can tell me how to pronounce all these words. All while we eat—P'Bau, what did you call this again?"

"Khanom khrok," she said. "You like?"

"It's delicious."

"I bring more. For children too." Happy, she scurried off toward the house.

"I adore her khanom khrok," Adrien said. "No one makes it better. All right, where did we leave off on the list?"

Hugh sat back at the table, Adrien tucked in against his side. He had nothing but time, his lover, and good snacks in front of him.

Life couldn't get any better than this.

Epilogue

After two days of being in Bangkok, Julian understood why Adrien adored it so. The city just had so much to do, and it was lush and beautiful. He knew very, very limited Thai, but the people were delighted he was learning their language and helped teach him. Julian did his best to be respectful to people, to good effect.

Also, seeing his master utterly relaxed was a very fine thing. Adrien had stripped down with Julian and Mac, towing them into the river and teaching them how to swim. Julian had caught the hang of it and was sure he wasn't going to drown if accidentally knocked out of a boat, and that gave him more courage to explore his surroundings.

Truly, he was quite loath to return to stuffy England so quickly, but Adrien had a case upcoming, so they had no choice in the matter. His master had promised them a lengthier stay after the case was done, and after monsoon season—something all looked forward to. Julian could admit he was a bit tired, hopping around the globe as they had over the past few months, but he had no complaints. It had been far too much fun to complain about.

Julian regretfully put full trousers and a shirt back on. He said regretfully because the Thai dress was far more fun to wear. From outside his bedroom, he could hear a loud pounding at the front door to Adrien's flat. Was someone here? What remarkable timing; they'd barely been home twenty minutes.

Raised voices sounded from the front of the flat, and that didn't herald anything good.

Darby went on the alert, going into guard position, and growled low.

Uh-oh. His dog adored people in general, happy to meet everyone. If she was reacting like this, then it must be someone very, very bad indeed. He trusted his dog's instincts.

Alarmed, he threw the bedroom door open and sprinted for

the front room, where the raised voices—two being his master's and Hugh's—were coming from. Darby raced ahead of him.

An angry male voice he didn't recognize was at full volume and could be clearly heard. "—won't have any son of mine going against me! It's obvious throughout the *town* what you've done, how disrespectful you are to me, and I won't stand for it!"

Adrien replied, his tone a drawl, but Julian had never heard his master more angry. "If you'd cared as much for your children as you do your reputation, we wouldn't even be having this conversation."

"You're the fucking faggot, and you've betrayed how I raised you!"

"*You* didn't raise me at all. You threw me at tutors and my master and ignored me for eighteen years. I really don't understand why you think I would have any loyalty or familial affection for you."

In that second, Julian rounded the corner and reached the opening of the parlor. No one was seated, with Adrien and an older man nearly toe to toe with each other. He couldn't see one whit of resemblance between the two, as the older man stood a good head taller, fair hair greying, face like a bulldog's.

Now, the woman standing in his shadow, she was another matter. She looked remarkably like Adrien—the same silky black hair and petite frame, her features a more feminine mirror of Adrien's.

Hugh stood right at Adrien's side, ready to take the battle to them, supporting his lover. Julian hadn't expected him to be anywhere else.

Even if Julian hadn't overheard the argument, he would know from the woman's presence alone who these two were. Adrien's parents.

Oh god. Adrien's father had hunted him down. Julian's fears had been right on the money, unfortunately. He'd known when that summons came in days ago that trouble was incoming, and Adrien shouldn't have ignored it. Now look where they were.

Darby growled low in her throat, staring up at the horrid man, her teeth bared.

It brought attention to the doorway where Julian stood, and Adrien turned about, realization dawning.

"Julian." Adrien walked quickly toward him. "Take Darby and

go find MacMallin."

Julian did latch on to the dog's collar, as she looked more than ready to bite Lord Danvers. (Personally, Julian felt he deserved it, but he didn't want to give the man any justification to put his dog down.) Still, he worried for Adrien, even though Hugh was there as well, glaring the parents down. "But Master—"

Lady Danvers seemed fascinated by Julian. "Is this one of them?"

"Shut your trap, woman," Lord Danvers snarled at his wife.

Immediately cowed, she ducked her head down, eyes on the floor.

"You'll watch yourself," Hugh said. "There is no need to speak to anyone like that."

"You're a damned bastard and have no right to—"

Adrien snapped around, temper flaring. "You either watch your tongue under my roof, or I'll curse you with boils! I don't know what you hoped to gain by coming here like this, but insulting any of mine will get you thrown out on your arse. I'm tempted to do it anyway."

Lord Danvers didn't take these rebukes well. He jabbed a finger at Adrien, face bright red in anger. "You think you can chastise *me*? I can have you thrown into a gaol! All I have to do is report your disgusting behavior and you'll be behind bars before you can even get a full sentence out!"

Julian's blood turned ice cold in his veins. That threat had the real weight of possibility behind it. Being homosexual in England wasn't a crime. It was the *act* of sex with another man that was criminalized. It was why Adrien had been relatively safe all these years, as he hadn't had a lover here in England. But his relationship with Hugh changed all of that. Lord Danvers really could report them, and neither man would have the ability to deny it.

Julian could lose the one man he adored and respected above all others to a prison cell and wouldn't have the power to stop it.

Hugh snapped at Lord Danvers. "Stop with your empty threats, you're scaring the poor lad."

With both hands on his shoulders, Adrien turned Julian about. "Go. Go fetch MacMallin, he's taking too long getting dinner for us anyway. Take Darby with you. We have this well in hand, I promise you."

He didn't believe his master for a second. Adrien, as always, sought to protect him. But Julian couldn't do anything by staying there, either. So he gave a nod like he would obey, grabbed Darby's leash, and quickly left the flat.

His dog whined at him, very unhappy to leave, and he shared the feeling utterly. He gave her a scratch behind the ears. "I won't just leave. I—"

Honestly, Julian had no idea what to do. Mac might have an idea, but he was just as likely to bull into that room and start throwing fists. Mac didn't really believe in talking things out, to put it mildly.

Who else could he call for help? Miss Stacey? Cynric? Neither had the status to overturn a lord, sadly, although they'd certainly come to help.

If only he knew someone with power—

Wait. Power.

He did know someone who had the power to stop this. Someone he could even call upon.

Turning frantically in the hallway, he looked for the nearest glass. Mirror, window, it didn't matter. At the very far end of the hallway was a window looking out over the street. Julian didn't hesitate, didn't pause, just ran straight for it. The second he could reach, he slapped a hand against it, weaving his call spell, and prayed the wards around the palace didn't prevent it.

Thankfully, they didn't, the call connecting smoothly.

"Prince Henry, this is Julian Danvers," Julian said, tone strained with his desperation.

"*Julian?*" Prince Henry's voice sounded startled. "*What's the matter?*"

"Your Highness, please, I beg of you to come. Lord Danvers—that is to say, Master Adrien's father—is here and threatening to turn Master in to the authorities."

Prince Henry swore strong enough to make a stevedore blush.

"Your Highness, I know you don't like him, but—"

Prince Henry cut him off, tone kind. "*I find him to be difficult, Julian, but I trust that man with my life. If he's in trouble, I'll help him. Now, tell me the particulars.*"

Julian sent another prayer that this wouldn't be a disaster and asked tentatively, "Do you know about my master? That he, um…"

"*That he likes men?*" Prince Henry finished bluntly. "*Yes, lad, I know. It's why his family disinherited him. Or I should say, why he left them. Is that related to the trouble now?"*

"Yes, Your Highness. Lord Danvers is threatening to turn him in, along with Master Hugh, if he doesn't nullify my adoption into the family."

"Wait, he has a lover?"

Julian nodded tentatively, even though Prince Henry couldn't see it, teeth catching his bottom lip. "He's been very good to us, sir. Hugh, I mean. Very good for my master, too. He makes him laugh."

"Peace, child, I won't cast any aspersions on them. What's this man's full name?"

"Sir Hugh Quartermain."

Prince Henry let out a bark of a laugh. *"Now that I did not expect. I know Sir Hugh. Damn good man, brilliant engineer. I've him to thank for us not losing half the population during the epidemic. And Lord Danvers dares to barge in there and throw a hissy fit, threatening the two of them, because Danvers adopted you into the family? The absolute gall of the man. All right, I'm now briefed. Where are you?"*

"Master Adrien's flat."

"And where's that?"

"221A Baker Place."

"Well, this is good fate. I'm rather close. Sit tight, lad, I'll be there in a jiffy."

Julian was shocked. He'd thought maybe Prince Henry would dispatch someone, not come himself. He was a very busy man, after all. "Is that all right?"

"I wouldn't miss this for the world, I assure you. I'll be there in a few minutes. Meet me at the front entrance to let me in."

Relieved, Julian agreed. "Yes, Your Highness. I'll do so."

He cut the connection, then jogged for the elevator. He wanted to be there before the prince arrived, and he never knew how long it would take the elevator to get there.

It seemed an eternity before it did come, and another eternity to carry him and Darby down to the main foyer. The second the elevator doors opened, he rushed through, only to check himself abruptly to avoid running a tall figure over.

"Jules," Mac said with surprise, latching on to the brown paper bag in his hands with the other hand, stabilizing his grip on it. "What the devil?"

Dealing with Mapinguari and Dogged Engineers 155

Julian grabbed him, mostly for comfort, as Mac was his steadying force. "Mac, something terrible is going on in the flat. Lord Danvers is here and threatening Master Adrien and Sir Hugh."

Mac's expression transformed from surprise to instant rage. "That rat bastard. I'll go—"

"No, stay with me down here. I called Prince Henry, he's minutes away."

"You called *the prince regent*?" Mac studied his expression, dark brows drawn together with concern. "What exactly did Adrien get threatened with?"

Julian glanced about the foyer, but aside from the guard at the door, no one else was about. Still, he lowered his voice. "Gaol, if he didn't strike our names off the family registry."

Understanding dawned and MacMallin swore, rough and low. His expression turned bleak. "But would Prince Henry be able to stop him?"

"I don't know who else can." That was the sad truth of the matter. He didn't know who else could stop Lord Danvers. True, a prince of a country should be able to, but if Lord Danvers made enough of a stink about this, he would surely tie Prince Henry's hands. It was a gamble, and Julian didn't know if that favor Prince Henry had offered him was enough.

From his peripheral vision, he saw a succession of three black cars with flags in the windows pull up. It was obvious at a glance that Prince Henry had arrived. Julian thrust the lead into Mac's hands, forcing his friend to scramble, shifting his grip on the bag to accept it, and darted for the door, intent on letting the prince in promptly.

Even as he sprinted though, he prayed. Prayed the prince could help. Prayed he wouldn't lose his home and master today. Praying was all he could do.

The guard at the door was utterly flummoxed to see royalty right in front of him. His manners kicked in after that startled second, and he gave a bow before quickly opening the door.

Prince Henry sailed through, strides quick. He was in an informal outfit—khaki pants and a simple white button-down shirt, boots coming up to his knees, his auburn hair swept back and glued down with pomade. It looked like he'd been going hunting or riding or something along those lines, which meant he'd not been on official business, and Julian was relieved about that. It would have just made the situation worse.

Julian bowed. "Your Highness. Thank you so much."

"It'll be all right, lad," Prince Henry said, sweeping him up with an arm and escorting him to the elevator. His blue eyes sparkled with what could only be called mischief. "I'll sort it out in ten minutes flat, no more."

Mac had had the sense to hold the elevator, a foot stuck in front of the door, and despite having arms full of food and dog, he managed a bow. "Your Highness. I'm MacMallin Danvers, Sir Hugh's apprentice."

"Ah-ha," Prince Henry said with a pleased smile. "Finally, I get to meet you in person. Pleasure, Mr. Danvers. Who's this?"

"That's our dog, Darby," Mac said.

The prince promptly offered a hand to sniff, which Darby willingly did, then bumped against his fingers for pets. He obliged with a smile.

"Beautiful dog. Well trained, too, despite still being young. All right, up we go."

They did so, and Julian was honestly confused by this, as no one else accompanied the prince. Didn't he need guards or a retainer or something of the sort? Then again, he likely had left everyone downstairs to make sure there were no witnesses to the conversation about to happen. And Julian was very, very thankful for his consideration.

Prince Henry kept scratching behind Darby's ears, which the dog loved, but his focus was on Julian and Mac. "Answer two quick questions for me. MacMallin, have you already started training under Sir Hugh?"

Mac was clearly surprised, but gamely answered. "Yes, Your Highness. We've been focused on building up the factories to process the manganese once it starts shipping from Brazil."

"So you're right in the thick of things. Good. Julian, what's the most complicated spell you've done so far?"

"Uh…" Julian had to think about that for a second. He truly did not understand to what purpose Prince Henry asked these questions. "I think the ward in Brazil? I assisted Master in creating a permanent ward around the worksite and mine."

Prince Henry stared at him for some reason, like he had to gauge Julian's sincerity. "You, yourself, used magic to build a ward with Adrien Danvers? In the middle of a jungle?"

"Uh, yes, Your Highness."

"Correct me if I'm wrong, but you've only been studying with him for about seven months."

"That's about right."

"My God," Prince Henry murmured, looking at him strangely. "He wasn't kidding when he said you're talented. Well, I can't wait to see what you two can do in ten years' time."

The elevator dinged, signaling its stop, and Julian was very glad for it. He wanted to return to the flat posthaste. He could figure out why Prince Henry had asked these questions later, when he had room to think.

As a group, they moved quickly to the flat. Even with the front door firmly shut, you could hear the shouting, and Julian winced as Lord Danvers grew even louder. Did everything he eat go straight to his vocal cords?

Prince Henry didn't even knock, just opened the door and waltzed in. Julian stayed right on his heels, pausing only to take Darby's leash so Mac had an empty hand to work with.

He could tell the very second people realized the prince regent was there, as they all sucked in startled breaths and the yelling abruptly stopped.

"Your Highness," several people murmured, sounding rather confused.

If a human being could look evilly delighted, Prince Henry was the embodiment of it. He rocked subtly back and forth on his heels, regarding everyone in turn. It did make something of a sight. In the fifteen minutes Julian had been gone, the center coffee table had been roughly thrown to the side, there were glass shards everywhere on the parlor rug, and someone—likely Hugh—had grabbed Lord Danvers by the neck, it seemed, as his tie was completely wrenched to the side. Lady Danvers was cowering in a corner as if to escape the violence.

"Your Highness," Adrien's words came out slowly as he examined the man. "What are you doing here...? Julian, did you call him?"

"I did," Julian said, not remotely apologetic about it.

Adrien slapped a hand over his face. "Shite. Julian, I told you I had this in hand."

"I don't think you did," Prince Henry said, grinning from

ear to ear. "And quite frankly, I'm glad he did call me. Now, let's address things from the top, shall we? Lord Danvers."

Lord Danvers straightened his tie and tried to look unruffled about a prince showing up in his son's parlor room. He rather failed as his temper still colored his cheeks. "Yes, Your Highness."

"I understand you object about MacMallin and Julian being adopted into the Danvers family."

Lord Danvers seemed to think the prince would be on his side, as he brightened perceptibly. "I do. Your Highness, surely you understand why—"

"I understand only that you're too classist and proud to be sensible." Prince Henry glared, a tic at the corner of his mouth. "My God, man, your pride is too costly. First you lose a son, who's one of the most powerful sorcerers in England, one I rely upon heavily."

From the startled jerk of his head, Lord Danvers was in strong denial that was the case.

Julian frowned at him, wishing he could shake sense into the man. That was right, even a prince could see how amazing Adrien was and value him. How his father failed to see it was anyone's guess.

"And now you want to throw not one, but *two* incredibly talented, brilliant young men out of your family. Did you not learn your lesson the first time?"

Lord Danvers regarded Julian and Mac with a confused, frustrated sort of expression. "They're just street rats."

Julian held his gaze without flinching. He was not "just" anything and he'd not cower in front of this man.

Prince Henry's head tilted back, an exasperated sigh on his lips. "You really are incapable of learning from your mistakes. For your information, Lord Danvers, Lady Danvers, the only reason why half of London is still living after the Spanish influenza is because of Sir Hugh, and it's why he was knighted. MacMallin is a star pupil under Sir Hugh. He's already apprenticed to him and is integral to the man's business, so that should tell you all you need to know right there. I have high hopes regarding that young man."

Lady Danvers seemed distraught, biting at her bottom lip as she looked at Mac. Julian suspected she had not come here willingly but had instead been dragged by her husband. She, at least, didn't look eager to back up her husband.

Lord Danvers, on the other hand, just looked embarrassed at being schooled by the prince.

"As for Julian"—Prince Henry was clearly not done—"he just performed a very complex warding spell in the middle of the Brazilian jungle. A *level four* spell, when he himself has only been apprenticed for seven months or so. If he can do this without even a full year of training under his belt, I can't wait to see what he's capable of in ten years. They're brilliant, truly talented young men, and you want to cast them out of your family? Understand that if you do, I'll quite happily arrange for them to be adopted into a different family and count it a good deed."

Dead silence.

Julian held his breath as well, hoping that would be the end of this.

Unfortunately, Lord Danvers rallied. He put his head back up. "But Your Highness, surely you don't condone their illegal behavior?"

Hugh and Adrien both had their mouths open on a hot retort, ready to lay into the man all over again.

Prince Henry held up a hand, staying them. "First of all, I really do not care who beds who. As long as all are consenting in the arrangement, it's none of my business."

Oh, good answer! This was why Julian liked Prince Henry.

"Secondly"—Prince Henry glared Lord Danvers into shutting his mouth—"if I were to go after every person in my country who has done questionably legal things, there's others I'd start with. I'm confident when I say that you, *my lord*, have far more to lose than your son."

That silence was back, this time with the air of thumbscrews and torture racks. All the high color in Lord Danvers' cheeks washed away, leaving him grey and shaken. Julian watched this transformation and wondered just what the man had done. Had he done something truly illegal? Prince Henry alluded to it, so he must have. And likely gotten by with it because he was an aristocrat.

"I think, unless you want to incur my wrath, your business here is done." Prince Henry waved toward the front door. "Feel free to take your leave."

Like a dog with its tail between its legs, that was what Lord Danvers did. Lady Danvers didn't utter a peep as she followed after him, eyes on the floor, clearly wishing to be anywhere else. Julian almost felt sorry for her, but she had chosen to marry the man and abandon her son, so this was a bed she'd made to lie in.

The second the door shut behind them, Julian felt like he could breathe again. "Thank you so much, Your Highness."

With some asperity, Prince Henry pointed a finger at him. "This isn't why I gave you that letter, you know."

Shaking his head in denial, Julian softly said, "By saving him, you're saving me. He's more than my teacher, Your Highness. He's the best big brother in the world, the father I never had, and the guardian I always needed. What else would I use this for except to save him, as he did me?"

"You silly." Adrien shook his head even as he came to Julian, wrapping him up in a hug. "You worry too much."

Julian hugged back, relief still rocketing through his system. He didn't care if this was the equivalent of firing a cannon to kill a fly. Adrien was safe, that was all that mattered. He could see the same relief in Mac's face and knew he wasn't alone in this. There was nothing they would not do, promise, or barter for Adrien's and Hugh's safety. To have this day end with them here at home, and not in a gaol somewhere, was all Julian really needed.

"I won't use your favor for this, lad," Prince Henry said. Warm blue eyes swept over the two of them, brow quirked as if he'd never in his life thought he'd see Adrien affectionate with someone.

"What favor?" Hugh asked, coming to join them.

"I gave Julian a favor, to call upon at will," Prince Henry said. "This was not what I intended it for. I shan't accept it for this, as frankly, squashing Lord Danvers like the rat bastard he is gives me great delight. You, Adrien Danvers, are a different matter. In return for saving your arse, you now owe me a favor."

Adrien released Julian on a sigh, giving the prince a resigned look, as if the world might end today after all. "Of course you would call in a favor for this. All right, fine, what is it? You clearly have something in mind."

The innocent smile upon Prince Henry's face was not to be trusted. "I might have a *small* problem in Leap Castle…"

"Oh, for god's sake, the place that's so haunted no one can live in it?"

Uh, but they had a case already? Julian wasn't sure how they were now going to juggle two of them. Although Prince Henry's case would undoubtedly need to be handled first.

"Just a few ghosts," Prince Henry soothed, still grinning from ear to ear. "Perhaps a demon. At any rate, something well within your abilities, isn't it?"

"Have you finally gone daft?" Adrien snapped. "I'm not a demonologist, I'm a sorcerer. What the devil am I supposed to do about demons and ghosts?"

Ghosts? Demons? Oh dear. This did sound quite outside of his master's wheelhouse. Julian hadn't the faintest clue why Prince Henry would send them in, of all people.

But this he did know: it was bound to be an adventure.

Thank you for reading *Dealing with Mapinguari and Dogged Engineers*! Book three will be out later this year, so stay tuned for news!

Need more patient and loving engineers? Friends to lovers? Adopted family? Check out:

Fourth Point of Contact

Want more sorcerers and magic? Humor and long suffering white knights? Check out:

How I Stole the Princess's White Knight and Turned Him to Villainy

and its new sequel:

How I Took the King on a Bone-a-fide Quest of Piracy, Piemu, and Profit

And check out my Patreon HERE! for WIPs, sneak peaks, and goodies!

Books by AJ Sherwood

Fated Mates
Fated Mates and How to Woo Them • Fated Mates and Where to Find Them

Fortune Favors the Fae
A Fae Coin Transported Me Into Another World and Now I'm the Gay Holy Maiden*

Gay 4 Renovations
Style of Love • Structure of Love*

Haelan
The Magic That Binds

Jon's Mysteries
Jon's Downright Ridiculous Shooting Case • Jon's Crazy Head-Boppin' Mystery • Jon's Spooky Corpse Conundrum • Jon's Boom-Shaka-Laka Problem • Jon and Mack's Terrifying Tree Troubles

Mack's Marvelous Manifestations
Brandon's Very Merry Haunted Christmas • Mack's Perfectly Ghastly Homecoming • Mack's Rousing Ghoulish Highland Adventure

R'iyah Family Archives
A Mage's Guide to Human Familiars • A Mage's Guide to Aussie Terrors • A Mage's Guide to Wicky

Ross Young
The Tribulations of Ross Young, Supernat PA • LARPing • Common Sense Deserts Again

The Sorcerer's Grimoire
A (Non) Comprehensive Guide to Sea Serpents • Dealing with Mapinguari and Dogged Engineers

Unholy Trifecta
How to Shield an Assassin • How to Steal a Thief • How to Hack a Hacker

Villainy
How I Stole the Princess's White Knight and Turned Him to Villainy • How I Took the King on a Bone-a-fide Quest of Piracy, Piemu, and Profit

The Coronation • How Tan Acquired an Apprentice

<u>The Warden and the General</u>
Fourth Point of Contact • Zone of Action

<u>Single Titles</u>
How to Keep an Author (Alive) • Marrisage Contract

Books by AJ Sherwood and Devon Vesper

<u>Spellbound</u>
The Insanity of Reincarnated Mages and Amorous Vampires

Books by AJ Sherwood and Jocelynn Drake

<u>Scales 'n' Spells</u>
Origin • Breath • Blood • Embers • Wish (a Christmas novella)

<u>Wings 'n' Wands</u>
Dawn (a novella) • Ruins •Rise •Soar*

AUTHOR

Dear Reader,

Your reviews are more important than words can express. Reviews directly impact sales and book visibility, which means the more reviews I have, the more sales I see. The more books I sell, the more I can write and focus on producing books that you love to read. You see how that math works out? The best possible support you can provide is to give an honest review, even if it's just clicking those stars to rate a book!

Thank you for all of your support. See you in the next book!

AJ's mind is the sort that refuses to let her write one project at a time. Or even just one book a year. She normally writes fantasy under a different pen name, but her aforementioned mind couldn't help but want to write in the LGBTQIA+ genre. Fortunately, her editor is completely on board with this plan.

In her spare time, AJ loves to devour books, eat way too much chocolate, and take regular trips. She's only been outside of the United States once, to Japan, and loved the experience so much that she firmly intends to see more of the world as soon as possible. Until then, she'll just research via Google Earth and write about the worlds in her own head.

If you'd like to join her newsletter to be notified when books are released, and get behind-the-scenes information about upcoming books, you can join her NEWSLETTER here, or email her directly at sherwoodwrites@gmail.com and you'll be added to the mailing list. You'll also receive a free copy of her book *Fourth Point of Contact*! If you'd like to interact with AJ more directly, you can socialize with her on various sites and join her Facebook group: AJ's Gentlemen and her Patreon!

Printed in France by Amazon
Brétigny-sur-Orge, FR